D1502863

BABYSITTING NIGHTMARES

THE TWILIGHT CURSE

KAT SHEPHERD

ILLUSTRATED BY RAYANNE VIEIRA

[Imprint]
MAKE YOUR MARK

New York

[Imprint]
MAKE YOUR MARK

A part of Macmillan Publishing Group, LLC
120 Broadway, New York, NY 10271

BABYSITTING NIGHTMARES: THE TWILIGHT CURSE. Text copyright © 2019 by Katrina Knudson. Illustrations copyright © 2019 by Imprint. All rights reserved. Printed in the United States of America by LSC Communications, Harrisonburg, Virginia.

Library of Congress Control Number: 2018955722

ISBN 978-1-250-15701-0 (hardcover) / ISBN 978-1-250-15702-7 (ebook)

Our books may be purchased in bulk for promotional, educational, or business use. Please contact your local bookseller or the Macmillan Corporate and Premium Sales Department at (800) 221-7945 ext. 5442 or by email at MacmillanSpecialMarkets@macmillan.com.

Book design by Eileen Savage

Imprint logo designed by Amanda Spielman

Illustrations by Rayanne Vieira

First edition, 2019

1 3 5 7 9 10 8 6 4 2

mackids.com

Think you'll steal this book, my friend?
Heed this warning: Think again!
Those who kidnap books, it seems,
Never live to reach their dreams,
But disappear, like Vivien Vane—
Never seen or heard again.

THIS BOOK IS FOR THE LOST MOVIE PALACES
AND THE DREAMS THEY INSPIRED

PROLOGUE

THE WOMAN RAGED against her prison door, but there was no one to hear her screams. Her red gown swept across the stone floor as she paced the room again, twisting her long, white gloves in her hands. She sat down on the low velvet stool and stared into the mirror. Her makeup was streaked where rivulets of kohl-stained tears left muddy tracks down her pale cheeks. There was no sound beyond her own ragged breathing.

The flowers around her had long since withered and died along with any hope that someone would come for her. She had been adored, and yet the world had abandoned her. One day they would all regret it. She would sell her soul if she could, just to have a chance to make them suffer for what they had done to her.

An icy whisper hissed into her ear, trickling down

like poison: "Have patience. You will live to see your vengeance." In the reflection she saw a pair of golden eyes—falcon eyes—meet her own.

The woman looked deeper into the mirror and saw only bone white and the glimmer of a midnight sky. She closed her eyes and felt frigid lips press against her forehead, the cold like an icicle burrowing deep within her skull. Something slick and dry moved restlessly across her face and down her neck with a sound like reeds moving in the wind. "Now sleep, dear one. The hour of midnight will come to awaken you." Then the woman knew no more.

. . . . .

Somewhere a clock began to chime, each silver note moving through her like a vibration. The woman opened her eyes. She was alone.

She picked up a washcloth and faced the mirror, slowly wiping away her smudged makeup until her face was bare. Her right hand reached for a golden tube of lipstick: her signature color, Phantom Red. She carefully traced a cupid's bow, checking her reflection in the mirror. After all, if her face was to be the last thing her enemies would ever see, she had to make sure it was perfect.

CHAPTER 1

MAGGIE ANDERSON SHIVERED in the December wind and looked up at the broken lights of the Twilight Theater's faded marquee. "I heard that the reason this place has been closed so long is because it brought bad luck to anyone who ever performed here. Do you think it could really be cursed?"

Rebecca Chin grimaced. "I sure hope not." She pulled up the hood of her puffy down jacket and tightened the drawstring. "Because if we find one more supernatural thing in this town, I'm going to lose it. Seriously." She looked down at the chipped blue-and-gold mosaic tiles beneath her feet as if they were going to jump up and attack her.

Tanya Martinez pulled a gray beanie down over her short hair and flipped up her coat collar to protect her neck from the wind's bite. She huddled closer to the empty ticket booth and peeked inside its cracked window. "Relax. There's no such thing as a curse. Just ask science."

Clio Carter-Peterson's hazel eyes sparkled. "No such thing, huh? Now, when have I heard you say that before?" She gave Tanya a friendly bump with her shoulder.

A sheepish smile spread across Tanya's face. "Fine. Let's just say I've never seen any evidence that would make me believe in curses."

Maggie reached into the pockets of her furry pink coat and pulled out a pair of fluffy white mittens. "Really? What about the Hope Diamond? Horrible things happened to anyone who ever owned it."

"Not exactly. Journalists in the 1800s made up the whole Hope Diamond curse story just to sell newspapers."

"Ugh. Fine. Then what about King Tut?"

"King Tutankhamun, you mean? Half the people who supposedly died from *his* 'curse' after they found his tomb didn't croak until about sixty years after they opened his tomb."

Maggie screwed up her face, thinking. "Anybody know any other famous curses?"

Clio rubbed her hands briskly up and down the arms of her navy peacoat, trying to warm up. "No, but I'm about to put one on my auntie in a minute if she doesn't get here soon!" She pulled out her phone. "She told us to meet her here at three thirty, and she's already fifteen minutes late."

Just then the girls saw Kawanna's familiar turquoise Scout pull up and park in front of the old theater. Clio's aunt hopped out of the car and adjusted her burgundy wool shawl, a heavy ring of jangling keys in her hand. "Sorry, girls! I got hung up at the shop and I couldn't get away." Clio's aunt Kawanna ran Creature Features, a costume and curio shop where customers could find everything from antique jewelry to plastic vampire fangs. She also had the best collection of old books in town, and the girls had found a need to delve into her unusual library on more than one occasion.

Kawanna held up the key ring. "So, who's ready to see the inside of one of the grandest theaters ever built?" The girls followed her to a set of inlaid wooden doors whose carved brass handles were chained together with a heavy padlock. Kawanna put the key in the lock, but before she opened it she stopped and turned to the girls. "The Twilight Theater was built in 1929. Graham Reynard Faust, the man who built it, dreamed of bringing our little town of Piper, Oregon, into the limelight. He wanted to make the Twilight the crown jewel of the Pacific Northwest theaters, rivaling anything in Portland, or even Seattle. And in a minute you'll see why."

Kawanna pulled open the door, and the girls followed her into a cavernous lobby. A breath of stale air wafted across Maggie's face, carrying with it a hint of popcorn and old perfume. Kawanna turned on the lights, and all the girls caught their breath.

Maggie marveled at the peeling, vaulted ceiling that stretched three stories above her head. The faded red carpet beneath her feet led to a sweeping grand staircase and a multitiered fountain, dry now, dripping instead with cobwebs over layers of crystal. At the fountain's landing the staircase split, leading to long balconies with delicate curved railings that looked down over the lobby's floor.

"Theaters like this didn't just show movies; they were also designed for concerts, shows, and plays. The Twilight wanted to open with something really spectacular, so they chose one of the greatest plays of all time. The advertisement for it is still there." Kawanna pointed to a faded poster in a gilded frame near the front door. It featured a red sword and crown on a black background, and the opening date,

October 24, 1929, was printed in white across the bottom.

"Whoa," Maggie whispered.

"Pretty incredible, isn't it?" Kawanna asked.

"And this is just the lobby?" Clio asked, her voice hushed with awe.

Kawanna nodded. "If you think this is something, Li'l Bit, just wait until you see the rest. Can you believe the town was planning to tear this place down? I've been fighting to save it since I moved here, and we finally convinced the council that renovating the theater could revitalize the whole downtown area. It's not certain yet, but if we can raise the funds we need to bring it back to its former glory, then the mayor will agree to let it stay." She led them across the lobby to a set of cracked, red leather doors and pulled them open, flipping on the other lights as she went.

As they walked down the main aisle toward the stage Maggie ran her hand over the red velvet seats, some of which had tufts of stuffing spilling out. She gazed at the moth-eaten, starry-blue curtain that was drawn across the shadowy stage and the orchestra pit. Her eyes glowed as she drank in the carved balconies and columns that lined the high walls. Even the most dilapidated details gleamed with the decaying splendor of a lost era. "This looks more like a palace than a movie theater."

Kawanna nodded. "That was the whole idea. Back then these were called movie palaces. They were designed to sweep guests away from their ordinary lives and make them feel as if they'd been transported into another world. Hollywood magic in your own backyard! And believe it or not, it only cost a nickel."

Rebecca's jaw dropped. "A nickel?!"

Kawanna smiled sadly. "It was all part of the magic. And part of the reason that so many places like this disappeared. They're remnants of another time, and not everyone thinks they're worth saving." She brightened. "That's why we're so excited about our new partnership. The newly formed Piper Playhouse Theater Company wants to make the Twilight its home base, and they've agreed to make their first show a fund-raiser for preserving the theater! I've already signed on to be in charge of costumes and props, of course. And in the spirit of honoring the history of this beautiful place, we're doing the same production that opened the theater. I'm even planning to use the original costume designs! Isn't that wonderful?"

Maggie's heart raced. "They're starting a theater company right here in Piper?!"

Rebecca grinned and threw her arm around Maggie's shoulder. "Uh-oh, Kawanna. Don't say the *T* word. You know how she gets!"

Maggie tossed her auburn curls behind her shoulder. "Can I help it that I was destined to be a star, and our stupid school doesn't even have a drama club? What's a diva supposed to do?" She climbed onto the stage and stepped around a glowing bare light bulb that stood on a stand in the center. She stretched out her arms and struck a dramatic pose. "See? I'm a natural." The others laughed, but Maggie's face grew earnest. "You guys! We should totally all audition!"

"Not me," Tanya said. "I'd much rather be in there." She pointed above the balconies to a dark glass booth. "The old tech equipment must be so cool! Do they still have the original spotlights?"

Kawanna nodded. "And the old film projector, too."

"Why would you want to hide away in some dark little booth," Maggie asked, "when all the best stuff happens on the stage?"

"Speak for yourself," Tanya said. Her fingers

twitched, and Maggie could tell she was imagining taking apart the old machines and figuring out how they worked.

Maggie turned to the other two girls. "What about you guys? Wanna audition with me?"

Both girls looked at each other and shook their heads. "Theater's not really our thing, Mags," Rebecca said.

"Really?" Maggie gazed out onto the sea of empty seats, and when she spoke again her voice was wistful. "But just imagine what it would feel like to stand up here and see everyone applauding for you. Wouldn't you love that?"

"Not really," Clio said.

"How can anyone not want to be famous?" Maggie asked. "I want the whole world to know who I am." She stood up straighter and put her hands on her hips. "And it's all going to start right here on this stage!"

"I'm sorry to disappoint you, but I don't think the play has any roles for young people," Kawanna answered.

"Oh," Maggie said, climbing down from the stage. "What play is it?"

"It's . . . the Scottish play."

Maggie turned pale. "Oh."

"What's the Scottish play?" Rebecca asked.

"The one by Shakespeare. About the Scottish king," Kawanna said carefully.

"Oh! You mean *Macbeth*?"

Kawanna stiffened, and Maggie sucked in a breath with a sharp hiss. "Don't say that!"

"Don't say what?" Rebecca asked. "*Macbeth*?"

Maggie flinched, and Kawanna looked over her shoulder and made a brisk gesture with her hand, as if warding off evil.

"Why are you guys acting so weird? What's wrong with *Mac—*?"

Maggie clapped her hand over Rebecca's mouth. "Don't say the *M* word in here. It's bad luck!"

Rebecca's brow furrowed. She pushed Maggie's hand down. "The *M* word?"

Clio's face brightened. "Oh, I remember this, Auntie! It's actors' superstition, right? The play was supposedly cursed or something, and it's bad luck to say that play's name inside a theater, unless you're performing it."

Kawanna shuddered. "And it's serious business; we veteran actors are a superstitious lot. I've seen people kicked out for saying it!"

Rebecca gaped. "*Kicked out?!* No way! That's wild." She looked around the theater. "I can see why people might be a little superstitious around here, though. An empty theater is kind of spooky." The scant aisle lights and the bare bulb on the stage did little to dispel the dark shadows that pooled beneath the balconies. "Maybe it will be less creepy in here once you finish fixing it up."

Kawanna looked at her watch. "That reminds me; I have to meet with an electrician in a few minutes. Are y'all okay on your own?"

"No problem," Clio said. "We wanted to see the theater, but we'll probably head out since we've got a bunch of homework to do, and Rebecca has to babysit in a little while anyway."

Tanya looked sideways at Rebecca. "Let me guess. Kyle, right?"

Rebecca beamed. "Yup. Still the best baby ever." The others smiled back at her, and Kawanna gave Rebecca's shoulder a quick squeeze before walking briskly toward a side door that led backstage.

"I'll see you girls soon. And Maggie, you make sure you keep those girls in line. No more talk of the Scottish play. This theater doesn't need any more bad luck!" Kawanna left the door ajar behind her, and the girls could hear her footsteps echoing down the stairs to the lower levels.

"It really is going to be beautiful when they fix it

up," Clio said, taking one last admiring glance as they headed toward the lobby doors.

"Are you kidding? It's already beautiful!" Maggie caressed a gilded owl that jutted out from a column near the back door. "Look at this! I can't believe nobody wanted this place. Seriously, I would be *living* here if I were an adult! Like, this would be my bedroom."

"Yeah, but what if someone came over and wanted to talk about Shakespeare?" Tanya teased. "You'd have to move."

"Very funny," Maggie grumbled. The girls stepped into the lobby and took one last peek behind them. "There's something magical in this place," Maggie said dreamily. "I can feel it. I breathe the air, and I just know something wonderful is going to happen here."

"Magic, sure," Tanya said. She dropped her voice to a whisper. "Just as long as no one talks about . . . *Macbeth!*"

Maggie's eyes narrowed in anger. She turned to Tanya, ready with a sharp retort. But before she had a chance to say anything, something behind them caught her eye.

The glowing bare bulb on the stage flickered.

And then went dark.

CHAPTER 2

MAGGIE'S EYES WERE sparkling when she plunked her tray down at the lunch table a few days later. "I just got the most amazing text!"

Tanya paused midbite and put down her forkful of tofu. "What is it?"

Maggie pulled off her gold sequined beanie and tossed it on the table. "Guess who you'll be seeing at the Twilight Theater pretty soon!"

Rebecca's jaw dropped. "No way! That's awesome! So you got a part after all?"

Maggie flopped down in her chair and pulled off her neon-pink cardigan, revealing the oversized pug T-shirt underneath. "No, not that amazing, but it's kind of close. I got my first real babysitting gig, and it's actually at the theater! Kawanna said I can probably spend some time backstage, too, and get to know what it feels like to work on a real play."

"Oh, that sounds cool," Clio said. She pushed up the sleeves of her moto jacket and picked up a sushi roll. "And it's your first time babysitting solo. Are you nervous?"

"Not really. I mean, I took the same babysitting course you did, and I've helped you guys tons of times. Why should I be?"

Clio glanced at Rebecca. "No reason." Rebecca looked down, and Clio took a sip of her kombucha. "I bet you'll have the best time. Who are you baby-sitting, anyway?"

Maggie picked up her pizza. "It's for the actress playing Lady Macbeth. She has a little girl named Juniper, and I'll be taking care of her at the theater while her mom is in rehearsal." She folded the slice in half and took a huge bite.

"Oh, so she'll be there at the theater with you. That sounds awesome!" Rebecca said. "When do you start?"

"I'm meeting Juniper and her mom, Emily, at the Twilight tonight. Kawanna's going to take me, since she has to be there anyway."

"Man, that's going to be so fun," Tanya said. "And definitely let us know if you need help."

"For sure," Maggie said. She looked across the cafeteria and saw a pale boy with glasses and blue-streaked hair walk in holding a brown paper lunch bag. Maggie stood up and waved her arms. "Hey, Ethan! Come sit with us?"

Ethan Underwood smiled and headed toward them. As he slowly wound his way between the crowded tables, Maggie scooted her chair over to make room. "Make sure there's an extra spot next to Clio," she said with a knowing smile.

Clio rolled her eyes. "Give it a rest, Maggie. We're just friends."

"Whatever you say," Maggie said airily.

Ethan plopped his lunch bag down at the empty spot next to Clio and slouched into his seat. He brushed his bangs out of his eyes and wiped his hands on his black skinny jeans.

"Hey, Ethan," Tanya said. "How's business?" Ethan had a pet-care business called Snout of This World. He had an uncanny connection with dogs, and he had never met an animal he didn't love. He also had a similar connection with ghosts, but that side of his business hadn't quite taken off yet.

"I've gotten some great new petsitting jobs thanks to Clio getting me that gig with the Lee family." Ethan glanced over at Clio and blushed. He looked down at his hands and cleared his throat. "So, what's up with you guys?"

Maggie excitedly told him about her babysitting news, and Ethan's blue eyes brightened. "Cool! I've always wanted to get inside that place. Old theaters are supposed to be full of spirits!" He pulled a sandwich and chips out of his bag. "Maybe we can go on a ghost hunt one night."

"Ugh! No way!" Maggie said with a shudder. "No offense, Ethan, but the last time we went looking for ghosts with you, things didn't exactly go as planned."

"Well, yeah, but that was my first time ever trying it. I'm getting better," Ethan said.

"Let's hope so," Rebecca said, and everyone laughed.

Maggie laughed, too, but it felt hollow. She remembered their last brush with the supernatural and how close she had come to being trapped in the terrifying Nightmare Realm. She pushed the rest of her pizza away.

Tanya saw the anxious expression on Maggie's face and tapped her on the arm. "Hey. We all went through some scary stuff a while back, but don't worry, it's over. And I think you're gonna have the best time at the Twilight. Just imagine how much you'll learn from being around all those actors!"

Maggie relaxed, happy to have her mind back on her new job. "For sure. Maybe they'll let me help out on the play when I'm not busy with Juniper."

Rebecca checked her phone. "Oops, I gotta bounce. I have PE next, and Mrs. Hitchings gives us, like, no time to change."

Clio stood up. "Good call." She looked at the rest of the table. "You want to head out?" The other girls stood up, too.

Ethan grabbed his trash and pushed in his chair. "I've got art, so I'll see you guys later." He smiled at Maggie. "Have fun babysitting tonight."

Maggie pulled her beanie back on. "I definitely will!"

Ethan picked up his blue backpack. "Oh, but, uh, Maggie? Just make sure the theater doesn't turn off the ghost light."

Maggie laughed and started to walk away. "Whatever you say, Ethan!" She stopped. "Wait a minute. What's a ghost light?" She turned around, waiting for an answer.

But Ethan was already gone.

CHAPTER 3

WHEN MAGGIE ARRIVED at the Twilight Theater later that afternoon, it was a bustle of activity. The cast milled about the stage chatting excitedly, and sounds of hammering could be heard behind the half-open curtain. Maggie noticed Kawanna talking with a white woman with short, platinum-blond hair. Holding the woman's hand was a four-year-old girl wearing overalls and a hand-knit cardigan. Kawanna waved Maggie over, and Maggie hurried to join them.

The blond woman held out her hand. "It's wonderful to meet you, Maggie. I'm Emily Forester, and this is Juniper. Juni and I are thrilled that you can keep her company here while I'm in rehearsal." Emily gave her daughter a squeeze.

Maggie knelt down and unzipped her brand-new, leopard-print babysitting bag. "Hi, Juni. I brought all kinds of books, games, and toys. What would you like to do first?" The little girl peeked curiously into the bag, and her face lit up when she pulled out a book with a picture of a girl in a tiara and black mask tiptoeing across the cover.

"Ooh, you found one of my favorites: *The Princess in Black*," Maggie said. "It's about a princess who has a secret identity fighting monsters."

"It looks like we picked a winner," Emily said. "Juni's deep in a princess phase right now."

"That's cool," Maggie said. "Princesses have amazing fashion, plus they run entire countries. What's not to love?"

Emily beamed at Maggie. "Exactly." She crouched down and smoothed her daughter's hair while she talked. "Kawanna tells me you're interested in acting, too." Maggie nodded, suddenly shy. "I think that's wonderful! I was just about your age when I first fell in love with theater, and it's been a part of me ever since. Let me know if you'd like a backstage tour sometime."

"Really? Wow! Thanks," Maggie said.

Juniper tugged at Maggie's hand. "When are we going to read the story?"

Maggie grinned at Emily and Kawanna. "If you need to head to rehearsal, it looks like we're good to go."

"I'm so glad this worked out," Kawanna said. She checked her watch and pulled a measuring tape out of the pocket of her embroidered orange duster coat. "I have to take a few more measurements before rehearsal starts. We're not letting anyone onto the balcony for now, as there are a few loose seats that need to be repaired. But there are lots of other spaces in the building up for grabs if it gets too loud in here."

Maggie led the little girl into the wings, the backstage areas on either side of the stage behind the curtain. She picked her way through the clutter of old props and scenery to find a spot where they would be out of the way but where Juniper could still see her mother. After passing an umbrella stand full of spears, a plywood Viking ship, and a taxidermic bear, she finally found a cozy little nook with a dusty purple love seat. "Look, Juni! It's the perfect spot for princess stories, don't you think?"

Juniper climbed onto the sofa and sat back, her little legs straight out in front of her. She wiggled her feet, the toes of her shiny red mouse shoes tapping together. When Maggie sat beside her she reached down and touched Maggie's glittery, gold leg warmers. "I like your leg warmers. They're so sparkly, just like a princess would wear."

"Thanks!" Maggie said. "I love sparkly things."

"Me, too," Juniper breathed. "I want my whole world to be sparkle and diamonds all the time."

"I get you, girl," Maggie said. She held up her hand for a fist bump. "Sparkles for life." Juniper bumped her fist, and Maggie pulled her arm back and exploded open her hand. "Princess power!"

"Princess power!" Juniper cried. She giggled and lifted the cover of Maggie's book. Soon the two had their heads together, deep into a tale of Princess Magnolia saving the day.

They had almost reached the end when Maggie heard a commotion from the other side of the stage. There was a loud bang, and the hammering stopped. She heard one of the carpenters curse.

Juni's eyes opened wide. "Someone said a bad word," she whispered. "I bet he's gonna get in trouble with his mom."

Maggie tried to hide her smile. "I bet you're right." She saw the actors clustered around someone lying on the floor. She took Juniper's hand. As they walked onto the stage, she noticed the man on the floor was holding his leg; his face held a grimace of pain. She stopped. Maybe it would be better to keep Juniper from getting too close. "Why don't we go finish our story down where the audience sits?" She tried to lead the little girl away from the crowd, but Juniper pulled in the opposite direction, craning her neck to see.

"That man got hurt. We have to help him!"

Maggie gently led her away. "I think it's super cool that you want to do that, but luckily he already has a lot of helpers." Juniper's face fell, and Maggie had an idea. "Tell you what. How 'bout if you make him a get well card? I bet that would help a lot."

Juniper jumped up and down with excitement. "Yeah!"

Maggie led her down to the floor below the stage and pulled some craft supplies out of her backpack. "Check it out. Glitter crayons!" Juniper began drawing with enthusiasm. "I'll go find out his name so we can write it on the card."

Back onstage, one of the actors was bandaging up the carpenter's leg. Keeping Juniper within eyesight, Maggie walked over to Kawanna. "Is everyone okay?"

Kawanna put her hand to her forehead and sighed. "Carl will be fine; it's just a bad cut." She rubbed her temples. "And we're lucky that the actor playing Banquo happens to be a doctor. But it was a rotten accident, and it shouldn't have happened at all."

"What did happen?" Maggie asked.

"Carl was standing over there"—she pointed to where a beam of plywood lay across two sawhorses—"cutting some replacement wood for the balcony. He heard something in the rafters above him and looked up to see a falling sandbag headed straight for him. He jumped out of the way in the nick of time, but he lost his balance and cut his leg on the saw."

Maggie gasped. "OMG! Poor Carl. He must be so freaked out!"

"To tell you the truth, I'm a little freaked out, too. There shouldn't have been any sandbags up there in the first place."

Maggie gestured at the messy backstage area. "Maybe there were some just left over from before, like all this other stuff."

Kawanna shook her head and pointed up above. "See for yourself."

Maggie looked up into the fly space above the stage to see what could have caused a sandbag to fall, but the rafters were empty.

Had the falling sandbag been an accident, or was the curse real after all?

CHAPTER 4

MAGGIE FOUND HER friends at their lockers the next morning. Clio checked her reflection and adjusted the red beret she wore with an A-line denim skirt, striped top, and navy over-the-knee socks. A pair of lace-up ankle booties completed the look.

"Ooh, *très chic*, Clio! I like it!"

Clio pulled a berry-tinted lip balm out of her backpack. "Thanks! I found the beret at my auntie's shop."

"Your aunt always carries the best stuff," Maggie said. "I don't know where she finds it all."

Rebecca pulled a roll of blue glitter tape from the pocket of her puffy down jacket and slipped a few magazine clippings out of a folder in her backpack. She carefully taped the images to the inside of her locker door, sliding a few cupcake-shaped magnets out of the way.

"Cute new collage," Tanya said. "What's the theme? Cupcakes?"

"Animal cupcakes. See?" Rebecca pointed to the images one by one. "Hedgehog, lion, and look . . . this one is totally adorbs. It's a pig!"

Tanya crowded closer. "Oh, so cute! I love the pink marshmallow nose! That's one pig I might consider eating." Tanya's green T-shirt said FRIENDS NOT FOOD in big letters across the back. She had been a vegetarian since preschool.

Rebecca squatted down to tighten the laces of her quilted high-top sneakers. "Yeah, I found a great website about how to make cupcakes into all different animals. You can do the cutest cake pops that look like little shaggy dogs! That's definitely going on the vision board."

"Nice!" Maggie tugged at Rebecca's fishtail side braid. "And no offense, but I hope the first few batches turn out horribly. It's been forever since we've gotten to eat any mess-ups; you're getting too good!"

Rebecca grinned and popped the collar on her half-tucked chambray shirt. "Sorry, Mags. I just can't hold back this sweet, sweet talent." She shut her locker door. "Speaking of talent, how was the theater last night?"

Maggie told them about Juniper and about the accident with the sandbag.

"My auntie must have been so stressed," Clio said. "They barely got the town council to even let them open the theater in the first place, and then there's an accident on the first day of rehearsal? That's not good."

"Well, it's an old building," Tanya said. "It's natural to have a few things go wrong."

"Like sandbags appearing out of thin air?" Maggie countered. "I think it's the curse."

"Not the curse again," Tanya said. "Where did you even hear that?"

"Oh, from a little place called the internet," Maggie shot back. "Perhaps you've heard of it?"

Tanya snorted. "Oh, if you read it on the internet, then I guess it *must* be true," she said sarcastically.

Maggie folded her arms and jutted out her chin. "Well, for your information, I didn't read it," she said haughtily. "I watched a video."

Tanya laughed and picked up her canvas backpack.

"Okay, then, in that case, I *totally* believe it," she said, rolling her eyes. "See you guys later!" She headed down the hall toward the science wing.

"You know you're never going to convince her," Clio said. "I don't know why you keep trying."

"I'll wear her down eventually." Maggie yanked at the hem of her leopard-print miniskirt, making sure it hung straight over the neon-pink leggings she wore underneath.

"But everything went okay with babysitting, right?" Rebecca asked. "You know you can always call us if something goes wrong, or if you have any questions."

"I know," Maggie said impatiently. "But nothing went wrong. It was totally fine!"

"No, yeah, I know it was awesome. I just meant, like, in the future."

"Yeah, duh, Becks. I got it. I know how to use a phone, okay?"

Clio closed her locker. "Let's get back to the good stuff. What about the rehearsal? Did you get to watch some of it?"

Maggie's eyes grew dreamy. "You guys, it was so amazing. They were just sitting around the stage reading their lines, and it was like the whole thing came to life right in front of me. It's like, you look down at a page of Shakespeare, and none of it makes any sense. But then these actors are all '*Wherefore*' and '*Hark*,' and I totally get it all of a sudden. How do they do that?"

"That's the genius of acting," Clio said, picking up her backpack.

Maggie shoved a pile of wrinkled papers back into her locker and slammed it shut with a bang. "I know! And I love it so much! But how am I supposed to learn anything when our school has no drama program? It's like we live in the middle of nowhere!"

Rebecca leaned against her locker. "It's a bummer. But in a couple of years we'll be in high school, and you can take drama there. Remember when they did *Our Town* last year? It was really good."

"But I don't want to wait 'til high school," Maggie whined. "I want to learn now! I don't see why we can't—" Maggie grabbed Rebecca's arm. "Wait a minute. I just had a great idea."

"What is it?"

"You guys, we're gonna have a drama club right here at Sanger Middle School. And I'm going to start it!" Without waiting for her friends' response,

Maggie ran down the hall, headed straight for the principal's office, her heart bursting with excitement.

. . . . .

"I'm sorry, Maggie, but that's absolutely out of the question." Dr. Gujadhur sat in his tall rolling chair, his palms flat on the tidy desktop. "I would love for our school to have a drama program, but we simply don't have the budget for it."

Maggie leaned forward. "What if I put on a talent show to raise the money? Everyone in Piper would come!" In her mind's eye she saw herself on stage, flowers at her feet as the whole town cheered for her. The mayor would hand her one of those giant checks, and she would smile for the paparazzi that would inevitably surround her.

Dr. Gujadhur's voice cut into her reverie. "We also don't have a faculty adviser. Or the space. And even if we did, a drama club is just too specialized to make it a priority. We don't have enough students interested."

Maggie's face fell. "Oh."

Dr. Gujadhur stood up and held out his hand. "But thank you so much for coming in. I applaud your gumption. Never give up, Maggie, and you can be sure your dreams will come true."

Maggie shook the principal's hand with vigor. "I understand, and I won't give up. One way or another we'll find a way to make the Sanger Drama Club a reality!"

Dr. Gujadhur looked flustered. "Oh, no. That's not what I meant. There definitely will not be a drama club here at Sanger, no matter what you do." He smiled encouragingly and ushered her out the door. "But don't worry, in a few short years you can join the drama program at Piper High School. I hear it's quite excellent."

"Why does everyone keep saying that?" Maggie mumbled. She turned to thank the principal for meeting with her, but he had already closed the door to his office. She stood alone in the hallway, her shoulders slumped in defeat. She loved acting, and in all her twelve years she had only ever wanted to be a star. Everyone seemed to think that she should be happy about something happening years from now, with all their dumb sayings like, *Good things come to those who wait.* No, good things definitely did not come to those who waited. Good things came to those who went out and found them.

Maggie walked down the hall, passing posters and flyers for school sports, chess club, and the math team. Why did her school seem to have plenty of money for stupid, boring stuff like that, but not for theater? One way or another, Maggie was going to get that drama program, and she wasn't going to wait until high school to do it.

CHAPTER
5

LATER THAT EVENING at the Twilight, Maggie found herself sitting next to one of the actors she hadn't spoken to yet. Alan Moseley was a tall, thin man with pale eyes and a receding hairline. He sat beside her studying his script, his long legs crammed up against the seat in front of him. He recited his lines silently to himself, his brow furrowed with concentration.

Maggie looked around and saw the other actors scattered throughout the theater, stretching, practicing, or prowling the stage as they waited for rehearsal to begin. Juniper and her mom weren't due for another hour, but Maggie had wanted to come early and watch. One man held a fake sword and practiced lunging at a cloth dummy that was hung from a hook near the front of the stage.

Maggie peeked back over Alan's shoulder. She cleared her throat. "Um, I could help you run lines, if you want."

He looked up in surprise. "Oh. Thanks, but I'm not quite there yet. I'm still on book."

"What part are you playing?" Maggie asked.

"Duncan. He's the king."

Maggie clapped her hands together. "Cool! That must be a really big part."

Alan smiled self-deprecatingly. "Not really. I get stabbed almost immediately."

Maggie looked horrified. "Whoa. I don't know if I would want to play someone who gets murdered." She thought for a moment. "Although it might be fun to die in a play. I would make it super dramatic!"

"That would be fun. The audience doesn't see Duncan get killed, but there are plenty of other parts that get to die gruesomely onstage."

"Really?!"

"It's a very stabby play," Alan said. "Tons of blood."

"Oh, wow. No wonder everyone thinks it's bad luck."

Alan laughed. "I wouldn't be too worried about that. It's just another old superstition that doesn't really mean anything."

"So you don't believe it? But you're an actor!"

Alan shrugged. "Actually, I work at the bank. This is my first play."

Maggie blinked. "So you're not, like, a professional actor?"

"Most of us aren't." Alan pointed at the man practicing his swordplay. "Jeremy over there is a professor at the college." He pointed to a petite woman with her gray hair cut in a bob. "And Helen is a retired zookeeper. Acting is just something we do for fun."

Maggie felt her heart sink a little bit. "Oh."

Seeing Maggie's face, Alan closed his book. "It's hard to make a living from acting, so lots of people who love theater work at other jobs and act in their spare time. But it doesn't mean we don't have talent. There are a few folks here who've done it professionally, like Kawanna." Maggie nodded. "And Emily was an actress in New York. She did a lot of commercials and TV shows, and she even taught improv comedy."

"Really?" Maggie asked. "I didn't know that!"

Alan smiled. "And I don't think you've met Myles yet. He's our assistant director. He spent his life as a working stage actor until he retired and moved to Piper. He's a real character and chock-full of stories."

"Wow." Maggie felt her heart lift back up again.

Alan pointed to a white-haired man striding forcefully down the aisle toward the stage. "Oh, there he is now." Myles Dubois had a pointy goatee and was dressed all in black and wore a beret and horn-rimmed glasses.

Irene, the director, hurried after Myles, her face etched with worry. "But Myles, you can't just quit! Please, we need you! You're the most experienced member of our company!"

Myles stomped up the stairs to the stage, his battered, expensive-looking boots pounding on the floorboards. His voice projected through the vast room. "I'm sorry, but my decision is final. I simply cannot work under these conditions."

By now everyone in the theater had turned to watch. Maggie plucked at Alan's sleeve. "What conditions? What's he talking about?" she whispered.

Alan frowned. "I don't know. Everything seems fine to me."

"Irene." Myles closed his eyes and took a deep breath. He slowly opened them, and his gaze raked across the audience of curious onlookers. "I had my reservations about taking any job in the Twilight, but I put them aside out of respect for you." He dipped his head and made a small sweeping hand gesture as though he was taking a bow. "But I was the first to arrive at the theater this afternoon, and it was dark." He paused for emphasis. "*Completely* dark."

Irene's green eyes narrowed in confusion. "I'm sorry, but I don't think I understand."

"You must know perfectly well what I'm talking about." Myles pointed imperiously to the bare light bulb that stood on a stand in the center of the stage. It was the one Maggie had seen flicker out on her first day at the theater. The bulb was still not working. "Everyone knows the ghost light must be kept on when the theater is dark, and *it wasn't*."

"*That's* the ghost light?" Maggie whispered to Alan. "What is he talking about?"

"Beats me," Alan said. "I've never heard of it."

Myles folded his arms and looked down his nose at the director. "Honestly, do none of you have any respect for tradition at all? Where's Kawanna? She'll understand."

Irene ran her hand through her short gray hair. "She's at town hall filing some paperwork. I assure you the light was working last week, but we seem to be having electrical problems. I'm sorry it wasn't on when you arrived today, but we've added it to the repair list we've given the contractors. Obviously everyone's safety is our top priority. We will be sure to leave other lights on in the meantime until we can get it fixed."

"Good God, Irene, do you think I'm some fragile old fool who's worried about stumbling over something in the dark?" Myles's voice boomed across the theater. "The ghost light isn't for *us*! And now that you've been careless enough to let it go out, I can only imagine the bad luck that's going to rain down on this place."

"Bad luck? Surely you're joking," Irene said.

Myles's fingers made a swirling gesture around his face. "Does this look like a face that jokes?" His steely gaze swept the room. "The ghost light is a sign. This building is cursed. And each and every one of us is cursed now, too."

The theater went as silent as a grave, and Maggie could have sworn she saw the stage lights dim.

CHAPTER
6

AFTER A MOMENT of stunned silence, nervous laughter rippled among the cast and crew. Maggie leaned over to Alan. "This is like a prank, right?"

Alan shook his head. "Myles Dubois does not play pranks. I've never even heard him crack a joke."

Myles bristled at the scattered laughter and disbelieving faces around him. "You really are a bunch of fools. I should have known better than to join a company of *amateurs*." His voice dripped with scorn. He flounced off the stage and into the aisle. "You mark my words. You'll all be sorry." Myles slammed through the door, barely avoiding Emily, who had just arrived. Emily jumped backward and pulled Juniper out of the way just in time.

The cast and crew erupted in a buzz of flurried questions. Emily slid into the seat next to Maggie, pulling Juniper onto her lap. "What was that all about?" Juniper waved to Maggie.

Alan leaned forward. "Oh, you know how Myles can be. He went on about some kind of ghost-light thing, insisted we were all cursed, and quit the production. You know, the usual."

Maggie reached into her babysitting bag and handed one of her old dolls to Juniper to play with. "Wait, so he's done this before?"

Alan's mouth twisted into a wry smile. "Well, the curse is new, but he's been threatening to quit since the first day of rehearsal."

Emily sighed and shook her head. "I hate to say this, but maybe it's for the best. Poor Irene was bending herself into pretzels trying to keep him happy." She gave Juniper a squeeze and kissed her forehead. "You ready to play with Maggie while Mommy goes to work?" Juniper nodded, and Emily slid the little girl off her lap and stood up. "Oh, and can you let me know if you happen to see my black leather tote bag around? I can't find it anywhere, and I think I must have left it here at the last rehearsal."

"We'll definitely keep an eye out for it." Maggie took Juniper's hand. "Kawanna said there's an old nursery downstairs, so I thought it might be fun to play there today, if that's okay."

"Sounds great," Emily said. "See you soon!" She and Alan picked up their scripts and joined the other actors gathered on the stage while Maggie led Juniper out into the lobby.

"The nursery is just down these stairs." Maggie held Juniper's free hand as the little girl clutched the tarnished brass banister and walked carefully down the carpeted grand stairwell that led to the Twilight's lower level. "Did you know there's supposedly a restaurant and even a ballroom down here, too? I haven't seen them yet, but if they're nice inside, maybe next time we can invite some friends and have a dance party!"

Maggie followed the sign at the bottom of the stairs, which pointed past a frosted glass door. "*Ladies' Lounge*," Maggie read on the door as she walked past. "I'm guessing that's just the bathroom? Everything was so much fancier back then."

The door to the nursery was open. Maggie flipped on the light, expecting to see a bright, cheerful space like the childcare room in the basement of St. Paul's, the church where she went with her parents. Instead she found herself in the doorway of a dim room with a low ceiling painted to look like the inside of a striped circus tent. The once vibrant colors had darkened to a grim mustard and maroon, and they met at a brass elephant chandelier hanging at the ceiling's center. The elephants' trunks arched out gracefully from the fixture's base, each supporting a flame-shaped amber bulb.

The circus theme continued in the dingy murals along the walls, where leering clowns and acrobats swung from trapezes and leaped through flaming rings. Painted crowds looked on, their mouths gaping in perfect, round Os of wonderment. A sad bear on a bicycle made his unsteady way across an open field, and a monkey in a tutu crouched atop a sway-backed horse that jumped listlessly over a hurdle. "Jeez, this is a one-way ticket to Creeptown," Maggie said softly. "They must have had a really different idea of what kids liked back in the 1920s or whatever." She looked down to ask Juniper if she wanted to leave, but the little girl wasn't next to her.

A dollhouse replica of the theater sat on a low, lacquer table across the room, and Juniper knelt in front of it, fascinated. She held up a blond doll that lay on the stage. "Look! This one's Mommy!"

"Oh, so you want to *stay* down here?"

Juniper grinned. "Of course! Look at all these

toys! Can we play here every day?" She walked her doll across the stage and made it take a bow.

"Sure, I guess." Maggie ran her hand over an open crate filled with neatly stacked wooden blocks and peered into a bin of tin trucks. She picked up a dented red fire engine and spun one wheel. The wheel squealed as it turned on its axle, and Maggie dropped it back in the bin. She wandered over to a puppet theater next to a cloudy, wall-mounted mirror in the corner. The puppet theater's painted curtain matched the one upstairs: midnight blue with sparkling silver stars. A few puppets sagged over the edge, and Maggie lifted the head of the nearest one and brushed aside the sticky, coarse hair to reveal a grotesque face with a ruddy, bulbous nose and pointed chin. "OMG, nightmare alert!" she cried, dropping the puppet like a hot pan. "Seriously. What was *wrong* with people back then?"

Near the dollhouse Maggie spied a wicker basket with a few holes in its sides. She bent over and peeked in, but she recoiled quickly at the musty smell emanating from the shredded stuffed animals tucked inside. "Oh, gross! I think the mice might have taken this one over." She picked it up and held it at arm's length. "I'm just going to go dump the whole thing in the trash can in the lobby. Do you want to come with me?"

Juniper didn't answer. She had found another doll, this one with dark hair and a beard. She sang to herself, dancing both dolls across the stage. Maggie put the basket down and tapped the little girl on the shoulder. "Juni."

The little girl barely looked up, still focused on the dolls. "Yeah?"

"I said I'm going to go throw this away. Will you be okay playing here for a minute, or do you want to come with me?"

"I want to stay here. I'm busy," Juniper answered.

"Okay, Juni, you do you. I'll be right back." Maggie left the nursery door open and carried the basket gingerly in front of her. "Please don't let there still be mice living in here," she said under her breath as she trotted up the stairs. "Or worse . . . rats!" The lobby was quiet, and Maggie made a beeline for the nearest trash can, lifted up the top, and dumped the basket and its contents inside. "Oh, grossgross-grossgrossgross!" She clapped the cover back on the trash can, careful not to look too closely in case there were a few squirming rodents at the bottom.

Maggie hurried back downstairs, her skin still crawling. "I definitely need to wash my hands." She popped her head back in the nursery. "Hey, Juni, time for a bathroom break. Let's go!"

Juni's back was to Maggie. She had put other dolls in the audience seats, and the blond doll stood in the middle of the stage. Maggie could hear the girl whispering to herself. She smiled, remembering being little and all the times she had been so caught up in her pretend games that a meteor could have landed in her room and she wouldn't have noticed. Maggie drew closer to hear what she was saying.

Juniper's whispering voice was sharp with intensity. "*The sleeping and the dead are but as pictures. 'Tis the eye of childhood that fears a painted devil.*"

An alarm bell went off somewhere in Maggie's mind. These weren't things a four-year-old would say. "Juni?" The little girl didn't hear her, and Maggie put her hand on Juniper's shoulder. "Juni!"

The little girl's wide brown eyes blinked and looked up at Maggie. "What?"

"What were you talking about just now?"

Juniper's face softened into an easy smile. "I was doing the play! Mommy was saying the lady's part."

Maggie relaxed, realizing the little girl must be quoting lines from *Macbeth*. "I know your mom's been practicing a lot, but you're a pretty smart kid to remember all those hard words, too."

Juniper shrugged. "She says them all the time. She's always whispering." She held the doll up to her ear. "Whisper, whisper, whisper. It gets annoying."

Maggie gently guided Juniper out of the room. "All moms can be annoying sometimes. Now let's go take our bathroom break and check on the rehearsal upstairs. We can come back and play in a little while, okay?" Juniper didn't really seem to be listening, so Maggie simply shepherded her down the hall toward the frosted glass door she had seen earlier. She swung open the door and switched on the lights.

The ladies' lounge was a well-preserved round room with a richly patterned carpet. The pink walls were lined with sixteen mirrored vanities built into gold-paneled nooks along the perimeter. Gold molding trimmed the creamy ceiling, and a small crystal chandelier hung from a rosette in the center. A thick layer of dust lay on everything. At the far end of the room was a doorway with a sign that said RESTROOMS. "Wow," Maggie breathed. "It's like being inside a jewelry box. Just imagine how pretty it will be when it's all cleaned up!"

Juniper ran to the center of the room and twirled, giggling as she watched herself reflected in the mirrors that surrounded her. "Hang on," Maggie said, and ushered the little girl through to the long hall of marble-floored restrooms. Instead of stalls, the toilets were tucked into tiny compartments with pink doors that stretched from floor to ceiling. Maggie's footsteps echoed as she checked the compartments until she found one with toilet paper and a door that could open and close easily. "Okay, here you go. I'll see you at the sinks in a second. Let me know if you need any help."

The sink room had black marble walls and yellow sinks, and the cracked tile floors were a simple geometric mosaic. Juniper came skipping in a moment later. "This is the prettiest, prettiest," she sang.

"For sure, Juni. I can't even decide which part I like best, but I think maybe the room with all the mirrors."

"Me, too! It's so pretty, pretty, pretty," Juniper sang as she pranced and spun her way through the lounge. She sat down at one of the vanities and made faces in the mirror. "Let's pretend we're fancy ladies getting ready!" She leaned forward and pursed her lips at her reflection. "I am very fancy, and I must get ready," she said, her voice deepening. "I must have my diamonds and jewels!"

Maggie sat at the vanity next to her and imagined what it must have felt like to have been a guest at the theater the night it opened, when the lounge was crowded with elegant women in gorgeous clothes, powdering their noses or doing whatever ladies did back then. She pulled open the vanity's drawer and discovered a golden lipstick tube and matching compact inside, each monogrammed with a *V*. "Cool! Look what I found!" She looked at the tube's label, PHANTOM RED, and unscrewed the lid to reveal a waxy stick in deep vermilion. The lipstick had a rancid smell, so she quickly recapped it and put it back in the drawer.

"Watch me, Maggie!" Juniper was back in the center of the room, twirling with dizzying speed. She pointed at the mirrors as she spun. "Look! Junis everywhere!"

Maggie laughed. "It looks pretty awesome." Juniper's pink dress and blond hair blended with the pink and gold of the room, and her reflection bounced among the mirrors, refracting like a kaleidoscope.

Maggie caught the scent of perfume, and she bent down to pick up a few dried rose petals she noticed on the floor under the vanity. She held them to her face, but she didn't smell anything.

Something in Juniper's reflection changed, and Maggie's eye was drawn to the mirror again. Next to the spinning girl stood a woman in a red gown, her arms encased in long, white elbow-length gloves.

Her face was obscured by a red hat and a heavy net veil.

Maggie smiled. "Oh, are they already doing the costume fittings?" she began to ask, but the question died in her throat when she turned around.

The woman had disappeared, and Juniper still spun across the floor as though she had never been there at all.

CHAPTER
7

JUNIPER STOPPED SPINNING. "What did you say?"

"Oh, sorry, I was talking to someone else." Maggie looked around. "Wasn't there a lady in here a second ago, wearing a costume? I thought I saw her in the mirror."

"Lady, lady, lady . . ." Juniper sang, dancing toward the door. "Lady in the mirror . . ." She hopped on one foot.

"Let's go back upstairs and check in with your mom," Maggie said distractedly. She glanced around the room. Where had the woman gone?

When they returned to the stage, Maggie expected to see Kawanna fitting the actors for costumes, but instead everyone was in the midst of rehearsing a scene while Irene and Kawanna watched with their heads together. Occasionally they would stop the scene, and Kawanna would hop onstage and move an actor to a different position, marking the floor with tape.

"They must be doing the blocking," Maggie explained to Juniper. "That's where they figure out where the actors will stand and move for each scene." She pointed to Emily, who stood to one side with Dallas, the actor playing Macbeth. Emily saw them and waved. "Now where's the lady in the red dress?" Maggie scanned the stage and the audience seats, but she didn't see anyone who looked like the woman from the lounge. She felt a ripple of uneasiness flutter in her stomach, but she pushed it away. The theater was full of people coming and going and changing in and out of costumes. It could have been anyone. *Or maybe I just thought I saw her*, Maggie told herself. *I bet it was just my imagination*. She took a deep breath. *Or at least I hope it was.*

Maggie unfolded two seats and settled in next to Juniper. "How about another princess story?" she asked.

Juniper made a fist and exploded it outward. "Princess power!" she cried, causing a few actors to glance into the audience.

"That's right, princess power!" Maggie said softly, exploding her fist, too. "I love strong, fierce princesses, but remember, sometimes even warrior princesses have to use their quiet inside voices, especially when their moms are busy working."

Juniper nodded, her eyes wide. "Okay," she whispered. "I'll use my quiet inside voice, too."

"Great idea." Maggie opened up the book and started a new story about a princess who went on an adventure to save her sister, and Juniper was quickly entranced. She cuddled up and rested her head against Maggie's arm.

After a few pages Juniper had dozed off, so Maggie quietly closed the book and settled back in her chair, soaking in the rehearsal. Emily and Dallas were alone onstage, and the other actors watched from the wings. Dallas held a wooden dagger in his hand. Maggie wasn't sure what was going on, but it seemed like they were arguing about killing someone. "Wow, it really is a stabby play," Maggie whispered to herself.

Maggie could tell that Emily was good. She made Lady Macbeth seem so murderous and evil that Maggie couldn't believe this was the same cheerful person who twirled Juni around until the two of them collapsed in giggles. How did she do that?

Maggie didn't know, but she hoped that someday she could learn to be as good as Emily.

Maggie thought back to her unsuccessful meeting with Dr. Gujadhur. There must be some way to change the principal's mind. He seemed to think that Maggie was the only person in the school who cared about drama, but she was sure there were lots of other kids who would want to join a drama club if only they had the opportunity. How could she convince him of that? Maggie turned the problem over in her mind. Suddenly, she remembered something. When her cousin, August, started middle school in California the students there weren't allowed to keep anything in their lockers. When the administrators refused to change the policy, August had circulated a petition around the school, and lots of students had signed it. Maybe if she started a petition, it would show how many other kids wanted a drama program, and then Dr. Gujadhur would have to listen.

Maggie pulled a purple glitter gel pen out of her backpack and scrounged around for something to write on. She finally settled on an old math test she found crumpled at the bottom. Ignoring all the red marks on the front, she turned it over and smoothed it as best she could. She wrote the heading in puffy bubble letters: *Petition To-Do List*. "Okay," she whispered, "here we go." She realized she had no idea how to start a petition, but she was pretty sure there were clipboards involved. She drew a heart-shaped bullet point and wrote *Get clipboards* next to it. She thought for a second and added a second heart-shaped bullet point: *Get pens*. After all, people couldn't sign a petition without pens. And paper. She would definitely need that. She added *Paper* to the list.

"Okay, good start," she said to herself. After a second she added her final bullet point: *Google how to write a petition*. She nodded in satisfaction, folded the list in half, and shoved it into her backpack. She could already picture herself standing in front of the school, maybe with a megaphone, rallying everyone to her cause. She would be wearing something fierce, but serious. Maybe a polka-dot kerchief and coveralls, like the Rosie the Riveter poster in her mom's office, but probably with a little more sparkle. Kids would be applauding and shouting encouragement, and she would lead them on a march straight to Dr. Gujadhur's office. Her petition would have so many signatures they would run out of paper. It was going to be awesome.

She grinned when she heard her phone buzz.

She couldn't wait to tell her friends about the amazing petition idea.

> How is rehearsal going?

Maggie almost dropped the phone when she saw the ghost emoji, her mind yanked back to the vanishing woman in the ladies' lounge. How had Clio known?

> Watching it RN. Emily's really good! Why the ghost?

> Idk. Isn't there a ghost in the play?

Maggie started to text back: *Something really weird happened*, but after a moment, she deleted it without sending. She didn't know why, but she felt strange about telling the other girls about the uneasy feeling the encounter had given her. She remembered how Tanya had teased her about the *Macbeth* superstition, or the way Rebecca and Clio had exchanged a look when Maggie said she was babysitting. Maybe she was imagining it, but it felt almost like they didn't quite trust her to keep a level head. Instead, she just wrote:

> Oh yeah!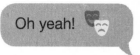

> Everything ok with babysitting?
> Need any help?

Maybe she wasn't imagining it. Maggie found herself gritting her teeth when she wrote back.

> Nope. Totally crushing it

> Tanya says look out for the curse lol

> Lol

Maggie didn't really think it was funny at all. She shoved her phone into the bottom of her bag and went back to watching the rehearsal. Emily was alone onstage, practicing a monologue. Her voice was clear and resonated through the room. Maggie wasn't sure what was happening in the play, but she let the words wash over her. *"They met me in the day of success . . ."*

Maggie caught the scent of perfume, and from behind her, she heard another voice, this one a soft whisper, reciting the lines along with Emily. *". . . and I have learned by the perfectest report . . ."* Maggie twisted around in her seat, but the rows behind her were too dark to see anyone.

Emily faltered and stopped, forgetting her line, but the hissing voice continued, dripping with venom, *". . . they have more in them than mortal knowledge."* Maggie looked at the actors in the seats nearby, but nobody's lips were moving, and nobody seemed to notice the other voice. Didn't they hear it, too?

The whisper grew closer. Maggie could hear it right behind her head. *"When I burned in desire to question them further . . ."*

It was almost in her ear now. Maggie could feel it, dry and hot on her neck, like a foul desert wind. The cloying perfume lay thick in the air like a weight. *". . . they made themselves air, into which . . ."*

Something touched her neck. Maggie whirled around. *". . . they vanished."*

The row behind her was empty.

CHAPTER
8

THE NEXT DAY at school, Maggie found herself avoiding her friends. She hadn't planned to, but when she walked through the front doors and saw them standing together at their lockers, she ducked down a side hallway. Last night at the theater had left her shaken and scared.

Maggie was terrible at keeping secrets, and she knew she would spill all her worries the second she saw them. Right now she wasn't sure she was ready to do that. She could tell that the other girls weren't totally convinced that Maggie would make a good babysitter, and if she admitted how frightened she had been last night, they would doubt her even more.

In their past supernatural encounters it always

seemed like it was Maggie who overslept or broke something or made too much noise. Maggie who panicked and lost her nerve. Maggie who almost got trapped in the Nightmare Realm. She was getting tired of feeling like the screw-up her friends always had to jump in and clean up after. Maggie knew she had been doing a good job babysitting Juniper. She had kept her safe and happy during all the weird incidents at the theater, and she had even handled a potential rodent infestation! But if she broke down and told her friends how scared she had felt, none of that would matter. They would just see her as the same old hopeless Maggie.

Besides, the things she had seen at the theater were definitely weird, but she wasn't 100 percent sure there was a supernatural explanation. After all, Kawanna was at the Twilight almost every night, and she didn't seem to have noticed anything strange. Maggie wasn't about to give up her first real babysitting job and her chance of helping with a live theater production. If there was spooky stuff going on at the theater, she would have to learn to toughen up and deal with it. And until that tougher, braver Maggie emerged, she would just have to avoid her friends in the meantime.

Shortly before lunch Maggie ran into Tanya in the hall. "How was the Twilight last night?" Tanya asked. Her voice grew teasing, and she wiggled her fingers at Maggie. "Anything mysteriously baaaaaaad happen?" Maggie paled and bit her lip, and Tanya's voice grew serious. "Oh, no. *Did* it? Did something go wrong with Juniper?"

"Um, no. Not at all. Everything's great with Juniper. I just realized that I forgot I promised to meet with Ms. Kulkarni at lunch today to go over my math test. I'll catch you guys later, okay?" Without waiting for an answer, Maggie waved goodbye and hurried down the hall.

She decided to hide in the library, knowing it was the last place her friends would ever expect to find her. The only books Maggie read were for school, and she gave even those only a half-hearted effort at best. The librarian glanced up and straightened his bow tie when Maggie pushed open the glass door and scuffed her gold-studded flats across the carpet. "Can I help you find something?" Maggie shook her head. She stood without moving, not sure what to do next.

Maggie couldn't remember the last time she had been inside her school library, and now, seeing it again, she remembered why. She found herself in an unremarkable room with practical brown carpeting, orange plastic chairs clustered around octagonal, Formica-topped tables, and modular shelves crowded with books. What did people even do in here?

Maggie was starving, but there were signs all over the walls that said NO FOOD OR DRINK. Her stomach growled audibly, and she saw the young man glance at her zebra-print lunch bag. "Hiding out?" he finally asked, and Maggie nodded. "Follow me."

The librarian led her to a table tucked away in a corner where a few other kids sat eating their lunches in awkward silence. Maggie realized she didn't recognize a single one of them. Some of them had their noses buried in books, but others just sat quietly staring down at the table or their phone screens. One girl with dyed black hair, tan skin, and a nose ring sat slouched in her chair. Her heavily made-up eyes were closed, and she lip-synched along to the music blasting out of her headphones. Maggie wasn't sure, but she thought it sounded like the *Les Misérables* soundtrack. Interesting.

The librarian pointed to an empty chair, and Maggie dropped her backpack on the floor behind it. He put his hand on his crisp blue-and-white checked shirt. "I'm Mr. Gallaher, but most kids just call me Mr. G. Let me know if you need anything."

Maggie smiled shyly. "Thanks."

"You bet," he answered, and headed back to his desk. "Fabulous tights, by the way," he tossed over his shoulder before turning the corner.

Maggie smiled down at the pink and black rose-patterned tights she wore with a short pink skirt, white Beatles T-shirt, and jeweled black cardigan. She pulled out her chair and sat down. A few kids peeked curiously at her from the corners of their eyes, but nobody greeted her. She slowly pulled out her lunch; her bag of chips sounded loud when she tore it open. Why was it so *quiet*?

Maggie wasn't about to spend her entire lunch period sitting in silence with a pack of morose-looking kids, like she was being punished or something. If there was one thing she knew, it was how to talk to people. She looked around the table searching for the ringleader, but there didn't seem to be one. Finally she turned to the boy sitting next to her. His pale face was sprinkled with freckles and acne, and his coarse auburn hair stuck up from his head like a brush. "Hi! I'm Maggie."

The boy looked up from the scratch on the table

he'd been picking at. "Oh, um, hi," he stammered. "Uh, I'm, uh, Alex." He looked back down at the table.

"Nice to meet you," Maggie said. He didn't respond. "So, do you guys always eat lunch in the library, or what?"

"Pretty much," Alex answered, running his finger along the edge of the table.

"How come?" Maggie asked.

A girl with mouse-brown hair and thin, patchy eyebrows spoke up. "Are you serious? The cafeteria is like the seventh circle of hell."

"Really?" Maggie crunched down on a chip. "I like the cafeteria." She got to sit with her friends, check out cute boys, and watch middle school drama unfold at the tables around her. School was mostly boring, but the cafeteria was where all the exciting stuff happened. She wished she could be there right now.

She saw Alex and the girl exchange a look. A look that told her she had just said the wrong thing. Maybe Maggie wasn't so great at talking to people after all. Or, at least, these people. She turned to a round-faced girl sitting on the other side of her, her nose buried in a giant book. "Hi, I'm Maggie." The girl didn't answer. Maggie tried again. "What's your name?"

The girl sighed and answered like she was doing Maggie a favor. "Jackie." She went back to her book.

"What are you reading?"

Jackie snorted and wordlessly pointed to the cover, where *Lord of the Rings* was written in golden, flowy script. "Oh, I know. I mean, I saw the title," Maggie said, blushing. "I was just wondering . . . is it good?"

The girl looked up from her book. "You're asking me if *Lord of the Rings* is good?" Maggie nodded eagerly. Jackie let out a humorless laugh. "It's only, like, the best book ever written."

"Really?" Maggie asked, encouraged. "Wow. What's it about?"

The girl just rolled her eyes. "Google it."

Maggie looked down at her untouched sandwich. This whole library decision had obviously been a mistake. She thought longingly of the cafeteria, with its dishwater gravy smell and crowded tables of kids—interesting kids—shouting at one another and laughing. Cute Trent Conrad could be standing at her table right now, tossing his floppy blond bangs as he stole part of her lunch. She imagined all the fun conversations she could be having with her friends. Maggie missed them already, and it had only been half a day. She wondered when the braver, tougher Maggie would emerge and she could face them again. Maybe it had already happened? She turned her mind back to the Twilight, and she felt a twist of fear in the pit of her stomach. Nope. She was still the same old Maggie, so she probably wouldn't be leaving the library anytime soon.

She had no idea how to even begin facing the Twilight mystery on her own, so until she figured that out she might as well work on her petition. After all, none of these people seemed to want to talk to her. Maggie pulled a fresh sheet of loose-leaf paper out of her backpack and took out her purple glitter gel pen. She wrote *Drama Club Petition Notes* in bubble letters at the top of the paper and used her phone to pull up a website she'd found about the importance of theater education in schools. She drew a column of heart-shaped bullet points where she could write down important facts to use. Next to her first bullet point she wrote: *Improves reading comprehension*. She knew this was something that teachers really cared about, so adding it to the petition seemed like a good idea.

The girl with the headphones leaned over, her smoky eyes flickering with interest. She pulled out one of her earbuds, and Maggie could hear Éponine singing "On My Own." It was Maggie's favorite song from *Les Mis*. "What are you doing?" the girl asked.

"Trying to start a drama club," Maggie answered.

"Oh, cool," the girl answered. "I've been going to theater camp in Portland every summer since I was ten. Can I join?"

"Definitely," Maggie said, "if I can convince Dr. Gujadhur to let us start one."

The girl turned off her music and brushed her long bangs out of her eyes. "I'm Valerie," she said. She pointed to a golden-skinned, spiky-haired boy seated to her right. "This is Nobi. He's seen *Rent*, like, fourteen times."

Nobi nodded. "Fifteen times, actually. But who's counting?"

Maggie laughed. "You're so lucky! I only got to see it once, but I do have the soundtrack." She looked around the table. "Anyone else interested in starting a drama club?"

· · · · ·

Maggie was walking on air by the time she arrived at the Twilight that evening. Three other library kids wanted to help start the drama club, and Val had offered to print out the petition they had drafted together and bring it to lunch the next day.

She slid into a seat near the stage to wait for

Emily and Juniper. Onstage the set designers were painting a backdrop to make it look like a castle wall. When Maggie squinted her eyes the gray backdrop looked almost like real rock, and the green-painted moss on some of the stones made it seem old and castle-y.

Her phone buzzed in her pocket. She hadn't looked at it all day, and she pulled it out to see a long string of texts from her friends.

[Rebecca 12:06 PM] saved U seat at lunch

[Clio 12:10 PM] T says you have to meet math teacher? RUOK?

[Tanya 12:30 PM] LMK if you want math help

[Tanya 3:05 PM] Did U go home sick?

[Clio 3:10 PM] Y U not answering?

[Rebecca 3:30 PM] CALL ME

Maggie thought about what to write back. Finally she wrote:

Sorry! Working on drama club stuff
TTYL

She was hoping that would keep her friends from thinking that something might be wrong. Maggie stood up and looked around the theater. There were no mysterious women appearing and disappearing. No strange whispers. Maybe everything was fine. Maybe she had been worrying for nothing.

Emily arrived with Juniper in tow. When Juniper saw Maggie she broke free of her mother and ran over, throwing herself against Maggie's legs.

"Hey, Juni!" Maggie said. "So what do you want to do today?"

"Can we sit and watch my mom?" Juni asked.

Maggie grinned, feeling a tiny twinge of relief. No spooky nursery today; she would make sure they sat right in front so they would be surrounded by other people. "Of course! You're pretty lucky having a mom who's such a good actress. Maybe you'll be an actress, too, someday."

Juniper shrugged out of her sparkly purple backpack and dumped it on the floor. She rummaged through her bag and pulled out a coloring book and some crayons. "Look what I brought! Princesses!" Her coloring book featured princesses from all over the world, wearing everything from hijabs to kimonos to long Western gowns.

Emily looked a little embarrassed. "She's still really fixated on this whole princess thing. I hope you don't mind."

Maggie's eyes widened. "Are you kidding? I basically made my parents call me Ariel for almost all of preschool. I'm still not convinced I wasn't born a mermaid."

Emily laughed. "I'm glad you understand. We definitely lucked out when we found you as a babysitter."

"Thanks! I feel pretty lucky, too." Maggie blushed. "I'm already learning so much about acting just from being here."

Emily smiled. "That's great! Don't forget that you're welcome at rehearsal anytime, even on the nights that Juniper's at home with her dad. And if you ever have questions, I'm always happy to help. I used to be a drama teacher, you know." She winked at Maggie and hurried onstage to join the other actors. Maggie's heart leaped. Could today get any better?

Maggie and Juniper settled in, Juniper happily coloring in her princess book while Maggie watched the actors stride across the stage, reciting their lines. The story came alive, and she found herself riveted to find out what would happen to the power-mad Macbeth and his scheming wife.

The tech crew was working on the lighting cues, and Maggie was amazed at how much atmosphere the moody lighting brought to the story. Emily's sleepwalking scene was cast in a cool, blue light, and Maggie could barely see the other actors. Then Emily glided on and the theater's old spotlight followed her as she paced the stage, giving her an unearthly glow.

The spotlight swung away from Emily. The actors continued the scene in semidarkness, used to the early errors of techs learning the new lighting cues. The pool of light skidded along the curtain and zigzagged wildly along the wall. Maggie giggled. What was going on?

Next to her, Juniper was tunelessly singing to

herself, hard at work coloring in a princess gown. She had worn her red crayon down almost to a nub.

The spotlight went black, and Maggie heard the director, Irene, sigh in frustration. "Cut," she cried. She turned and squinted into the lighting catwalk. "What's going on up there, Oliver?"

"Sorry, I'm just having trouble with this old light!" a male voice called down. "It looks like the bulb burnt out. I'll go grab a new one from the storeroom." Oliver flipped on the other stage lights, and Maggie heard the clang of his heavy boots as he trotted along the catwalk and down the ladder.

Irene stretched. "Okay, everybody. Take five." The actors relaxed.

Kawanna tapped Emily on the shoulder. "Can I grab you for a few minutes? I finished altering your costume, and I want to check it for fit." The two of them disappeared backstage.

A moment later Maggie heard cries of dismay coming from the wings. Kawanna and Emily rushed back to the stage, and Kawanna carried a bundle of fabric in her arms. "Irene!" Kawanna cried. "Can you come take a look at this?" Irene hurried over, and the three of them clustered together, their voices tight and hushed.

"Can I have everyone's attention for a moment?" The cast and crew gathered around Irene. "Has anyone been near the dressing rooms today?" The actors and crew members shook their heads. "No one was sawing back there, or using any of the carpentry equipment?" The folks onstage gave confused denials, and Maggie wondered what was going on. Why would the director ask that? Irene's voice grew frustrated. "And nobody saw anyone walking around back there?"

Dallas's voice rose above the confused murmurs of his castmates. "Irene, we're kind of in the dark here. What happened?"

Kawanna let the bunched-up fabric in her hands drop, and Maggie could see it was a long gown, but something about it looked off. "It's Emily's costume." She stretched out part of the skirt. "Or at least it was. It's been slashed to ribbons."

The room exploded with cries of shock. Everyone started talking at once, their voices growing louder as they pushed forward to get a closer look at the damaged costume. Maggie was stunned. Emily was so nice. Maggie couldn't imagine anyone wanting to destroy her costume on purpose.

"Oh, your mom's poor costume! I wonder how it happened."

Juniper barely raised her eyes from her coloring page. "*She* did it."

"What? Who did it?"

Juniper finally lifted her head to stare at one of the balcony boxes above them. Maggie followed her eyes.

Someone stood in the balcony box, her arms raised in triumph. Maggie felt her body go cold. It was the woman in red, and something silvery gleamed in her grip. The woman moved, and Maggie could finally see what she held that had caught the light. It was the long, sharp blade of a butcher knife.

CHAPTER 9

MAGGIE GASPED AND gripped the arms of her chair. The cast and crew were still in a flurry of concerned activity onstage. Had anyone else seen the woman in red?

Oliver returned with the spot bulb and flicked on the house lights. The balcony box was empty now, and the cast and crew were clearing the stage to rehearse the scene again. Emily stood near the wings while Kawanna retook her measurements. Nobody was talking about the mysterious figure in the balcony.

Juniper went back to coloring in her book. She still sang to herself as she colored, and Maggie could finally understand the words. "Lady, lady, lady. A lady all in red," Juniper sang. Her princess wore a red dress, and Juni had scribbled over her face in red crayon, too. Like a veil.

"Juni," Maggie said quietly. "Tell me about what you're coloring."

Juniper dropped the red crayon and picked up a dark-blue one. She colored the background in long sweeps. "You saw her."

Maggie swallowed thickly. "I did." She looked around at the other actors and lowered her voice. "Does anyone else see her? Where is she now?"

Juniper shrugged. "She's always here." Juniper danced her blue crayon in the air. "Always watching," she sang.

Maggie felt an icicle of true fear pierce her heart. None of the adults seemed able to see the mysterious visitor. Could the woman in red be a ghost? Or even the Night Queen? Maggie tried to make her voice sound light and unconcerned. "Who is she watching, Juni?"

Juniper picked up a silver crayon and made jagged dots on the dark-blue background, pressing hard. "Mostly she watches Mommy." Her voice dropped to a whisper. "I don't think she likes Mommy very much."

"Because she cut up your mom's dress?" Maggie asked.

Juniper nodded and pointed down at the coloring book page. She had drawn a knife in one hand of the red princess and a black bag in the other. "And she cuts up Mommy's other things, too."

Maggie remembered Emily's missing tote. "Did she cut up your mom's bag?"

Juniper nodded. She held up her fingers and ticked off items one by one. "And her scarf. Her sweatshirt. Her furry white coat."

Maggie's skin crawled, imagining the woman in red gleefully slashing up Emily's things. "Why would she do that?"

Juniper shrugged. "I don't know."

Maggie tried to question her further, but Juniper ignored her, coloring silently. Maggie found herself peering over her shoulder and jumping at every sound, afraid to leave her seat until rehearsal ended and Emily came down from the stage, her face and shoulders tight with tension. Emily forced a smile and tried to make her voice sound cheerful when she greeted her daughter. "Hi, Junebug." She looked at Maggie. "How was she today?"

Maggie wasn't sure what to say. "Uhhh, quiet, I guess. She was really into coloring in her book." Should she tell Emily what Juniper had said about the woman in red? Maggie opened the book to the page that Juniper colored that evening. "She was pretty busy making this. Isn't it interesting?" She watched Emily's eyes, looking for some sign that she understood.

Emily barely glanced at the coloring page. "What a terrific princess. She looks very brave and strong." She kissed the top of Juniper's head. "Just like you!"

"Juniper, don't you want to tell your mom about your princess?" Maggie asked.

"No," Juniper said simply.

This was going nowhere fast. "It's awful about your dress," Maggie said. "What happened?"

Emily shrugged. "Who knows? I'm sure it was just an accident."

Maggie sighed inwardly. *Great*, she thought. *Another adult who has paranormal stuff happening right under her nose and can't even see it.* Thank goodness Clio's aunt was at the theater, too. She would know what to do.

Emily looked back at the stage. "I just feel so bad for Kawanna, having to make a new costume when she's already so overworked now that she's the assistant director, too."

Maggie watched Kawanna onstage, writing feverishly on a clipboard as she spoke to the director. Maggie realized they had barely spoken at rehearsals because Kawanna was always rushing around somewhere. Her usually perfect nails were chipped, and she wasn't wearing a single accessory. The Kawanna that Maggie knew and loved was lively and fun, fashionably dressed and quick with a joke. This Kawanna looked frazzled, with bags under her eyes. And she hadn't played a single prank on the girls since she started working on the Twilight renovation. *Poor Kawanna. She must be really stressed.* What would she do if Maggie dumped yet another problem in her lap? *Nice work on the play, Kawanna. Oh, by the way, the theater's haunted by an angry ghost that keeps ripping up Emily's stuff.* There was no way she could tell her. Maggie would just have to keep going it alone.

· · · · ·

Maggie was intentionally late to school the next morning so she would have an excuse to avoid her friends. Seeing the woman in red wave a knife around had scared her more than ever, especially when she thought about Emily's clothes. But Maggie still didn't feel ready to ask for help. Telling them about her fears felt like saying *This is too hard for me.* It felt like giving up, and it would only prove everything they probably already thought about her.

On the way to the library at lunch, she texted Tanya.

> Meeting up w/fellow drama geeks 2 work on petition

> Need any help?

Maggie stared at Tanya's reply. It would feel so good just to tell them the truth, to know that she didn't have to try to fix this by herself. She started to type *Y-E-S*, but she deleted the letters before she sent them.

> No thx!
> TTYL

She slid the phone back in her bag without looking at the reply and paused at the library door. She was tired of thinking about the Twilight, and the drama club petition was the perfect distraction. She squared her shoulders and walked into the library, waving to Mr. Gallaher. He wore a green bow tie with an orange striped shirt and greeted Maggie with a big smile. "Welcome back! You look a little happier today."

Maggie smiled back. "Is Val back there already?"

Mr. Gallaher nodded. "She used the copier this morning for your petition. I think she's already gotten some signatures."

Maggie brightened. "Yay! I can't wait to see!" She hurried back to the table, where Val, Nobi, and some of the other kids crowded around a stack of papers.

Val looked up and grinned. "Nobi and I got about forty signatures each this morning!"

Maggie's eyes widened. "*Each?* Wow! That many kids want to join drama club?"

Nobi laughed. "No. I think they just like the idea of sticking it to Dr. Gujadhur. We're always having to listen to him, and it's pretty cool to make him listen to us for a change."

Alice, a petite girl with blue eyes and curly blond hair, picked up a stack of empty signature pages. "We should take these to the cafeteria. We can get a lot during lunch!"

Maggie hesitated. What if her friends noticed something was wrong? Then it would all come spilling out. *Wait a minute*, she thought. *I'm an actress.* She tossed back her hair and held out her arms for a pile of petitions. "Let's do this!"

By the end of lunch, they had a stack of signature

pages tall enough to impress the strictest principal. Maggie had even gotten Trent Conrad to sign! She smiled down at her friends' names signed in purple glitter gel pen: *Rebecca Chin, Clio Carter-Peterson,* and *Tanya Martinez*. They hadn't noticed a thing. She had been amazing. Maggie's smile faltered. But she hadn't liked not telling them about the Twilight. It felt too much like lying. Maggie pushed the thought away and picked up the sheaf of papers. She turned to Val. "Ready?" Val grinned and followed her to Dr. Gujadhur's office.

"Dr. Gujadhur, we have a petition to start an after-school drama club here at Sanger Middle, and we have over two hundred signatures." Maggie plopped the petition onto the principal's desk with a flourish. She felt like a character in a movie.

The principal sighed. "Ah, it's Miss Anderson again." He looked at Valerie. "And Miss Leo." He made no move to touch the pile of papers.

"Well?" Maggie said. "Aren't you going to look at it?"

Dr. Gujadhur looked tired. "As I've already explained, we simply don't have the resources to add a drama club. A petition isn't going to change that."

Maggie felt a rising frustration. "Why not? Before you said that there weren't enough kids interested."

She pointed to the signatures. "But look. Lots of kids would join!"

"Girls, I appreciate all your hard work, but my hands are tied." He reached into a tray on his desk and slid a goldenrod-yellow flyer toward the girls. "Perhaps you'd consider joining the chess club instead." Maggie and Val stared at it in disbelief. Dr. Gujadhur slowly slid a second flyer over the first one, this one a dull baby blue. "Or volleyball? I believe Mrs. Hitchings is hosting tryouts next week."

If she were in a movie Maggie would have crumpled up the flyers and thrown them back in his face with some impressive insult before flouncing out. But she wasn't in a movie, and Maggie didn't want to get into trouble. Besides, she couldn't think of any impressive insults. Instead Maggie and Val filed slowly out of the office, leaving the petition on his desk, untouched. "Don't forget, girls, there's always high school!" Dr. Gujadhur called after them.

Maggie was so disappointed she couldn't even look at Val. "Don't worry," Val said. "We'll figure something out." But it didn't sound like her heart was in it. The two girls shouldered their backpacks and headed to class.

Maggie didn't think she had ever felt so miserable. She had been thrilled about the new theater company and her first babysitting job, but instead of being wonderful everything was just one big disaster. The theater was cursed, her babysitting gig was scary instead of exciting, and she couldn't even tell her friends about any of it. And now her dream of starting a drama club had just swirled down the toilet, too. She felt tears welling up in her eyes. Could things get any worse?

CHAPTER
10

THAT NIGHT AT rehearsal Maggie could barely concentrate. Her eyes scanned every shadow, wondering where the woman in red would strike next. Juniper begged her to play in the nursery again, but Maggie made up an excuse, afraid to leave the safety of the stage and the first few rows of seats. She pulled out some board games and an activity book, managing to keep the little girl busy almost the entire evening. But after a while Juniper wriggled in her seat. "I have to go to the bathroom."

Maggie looked fearfully around the theater. "Rehearsal is almost finished. Are you sure you can't hold it?"

Juniper squirmed out of her seat and hopped up and down. "No! I have to go *now!*"

Maggie stood up and held out her hand. "Okay, but let's make it quick so we can get back here to watch your mom." As they walked down the steps to the ladies' lounge, Maggie found herself looking over her shoulder, cringing at the thought that she would see the woman in red following them. The phantom woman seemed mostly focused on the theater company, but that didn't make her any less frightening. The attack on Emily's things seemed so vicious. So . . . personal.

"Ow! Why are you squeezing my hand so hard?" Juniper slithered out of Maggie's grip.

Maggie dropped her hand. "Sorry." She pushed open the door to the lounge, keeping her eyes on the patterned carpet and not on the gilded mirrors along the walls. "Let's hurry up and go back upstairs." Maggie found two stalls next to each other and closed the doors.

A few moments later she heard Juniper's door open and her mouse shoes squeak across the marble floor. "Juni? Where are you going?" The little girl didn't answer. "Wait for me, okay? And we'll wash our hands together." Maggie heard only silence.

"Juniper?" Maggie opened the door and walked along the other stalls, searching each one. They were all empty. "Juniper!" Feeling a rising panic, she hurried into the washroom, but she wasn't at the sinks, either.

"The mirrors," Maggie said to herself. Juniper loved playing in there. Maggie ran through the doorway to the lounge. Juniper wasn't dancing in front of the mirrors. Could she be hiding under one of the vanities? Maggie dropped to her hands and knees and peered behind each chair. Nothing. Where else could she be?

The nursery.

Maggie ran toward the nursery. "Juni! Where are you?" She noticed a doll on the hall floor outside the doorway, and a wave of relief washed over her. Juniper must have wandered in here to play. Maggie rushed into the room expecting to see the little girl crouched in front of the dollhouse, but the room was empty. Her stomach twisted with fear.

She had lost Juniper.

Maggie's heart pounded in her chest. Where would Juniper go? She picked up the doll at her feet. Could Juni have taken the dolls from the nursery to another place? Wherever it was, she couldn't have gotten far. Maggie walked farther down the hall and noticed another doll on the floor in front of a thick metal door at the end of the hallway. A big sign said KEEP FIRE DOOR CLOSED AT ALL TIMES. The door was slightly ajar.

Maggie ducked her head in. "Juniper?" Beyond the doorway the hall was narrower and darker. The old lighting fixtures were burned out, and instead of the plush red carpeting and ornate wallpaper of the public parts of the theater, the floor was a cold, industrial tile, and the walls were covered in peeling gray paint. Maggie found another doll on the floor next to a few dried rose petals at the top of a dark stairwell. She hesitated. What if the dolls weren't left by Juniper?

Below her Maggie heard a familiar, tuneless singing, and her heart flooded with relief. *Juniper.* Maggie hurried down the steps as carefully as she dared, gripping the handrail tightly, and found the little girl alone on the landing. The second stairwell below her was in almost total darkness, but Juniper was about to descend, her arms too full of dolls to hold on to the railing. "Juni! No!"

The girl stopped and turned around, losing her balance. She teetered and started to tip backward. Maggie lunged for her, catching her just before she toppled down the steps. The dolls fell from her arms and scattered across the landing.

Maggie took a shuddering breath and hugged the little girl against her. "Juni, are you okay? You scared me! We were supposed to stick together, remember?"

"I'm sorry." Juniper started to cry.

Maggie comforted her. "It's okay; I'm not mad. I was just worried. I couldn't find you! What were you doing down here?"

Juniper sniffled. "I was playing. I was doing a treasure hunt."

"Sweetie, you can't play down here. It's really dark and dangerous, and it was hard to find you. You almost got hurt. If you want to make a treasure hunt, we can plan one someplace safer."

"No!" The little girl twisted out of Maggie's arms. "I wasn't *making* the treasure hunt; I was *on* it! I followed *them*." She knelt down and began to collect the dolls scattered along the landing. "It was like Hansel and Gretel and the trail of breadcrumbs."

"They led you down here?" Maggie asked.

"Uh huh. See, that's *my* name." She held up her favorite blond-haired doll from the nursery. Tied around the doll's neck was a red ribbon with a creamy card attached, edged in red. *Juniper* was written on the front in red ink.

A chill crept over Maggie's spine.

Maggie flipped the card over and found *Follow me* written on the back in the same red ink. The handwriting was graceful, with bold, sweeping strokes. Maggie held the card to her nose and inhaled. Perfume.

She knew who had set up the treasure hunt. The woman in red wasn't after Emily; she wanted Juniper.

When Maggie and Juniper exited the dark hallway, Maggie closed the heavy fire door firmly behind them. She knelt down in front of Juniper and looked her straight in the eye. "Juni, this is really important. You can't go down there again, no matter what. It's very dangerous. Okay?"

Juniper's lip quivered. "Okay."

Maggie brushed the little girl's hair out of her eyes. "And you have to promise me that you won't ever go off by yourself. I'm your babysitter, and it's my job to keep you safe. I can't do that if I don't know where you are. You got it?"

Juniper nodded solemnly. "Good," Maggie said. "Now let's put these dolls away and go find your mom. I bet she would love to give you a great big hug right now!"

Back upstairs the cast and crew were finishing

up for the day. Emily looked drawn as she hunted among the rows of seats for her things. "Let us help," Maggie suggested.

Emily forced a tired smile and swept Juniper into her arms, spinning her around. "How's my little Junebug? Did you have a fabulous princess adventure today?"

Maggie squeezed Juniper's coloring books and crayons into her sparkly backpack. "Maybe a bit *too* much of an adventure," she said carefully. She told Emily how Juniper had wandered off, leaving out the woman in red's role in it. "I went over the rules with her, but I think it would help if you went over them again with her, too," Maggie said. "It really scared me when I couldn't find her." She bit her lip and looked down. "I'll understand if you don't want me to babysit her anymore."

Emily's face softened. "Maggie, it sounds to me like you did everything right. Juniper knows better than to wander off on her own without telling anyone." She touched her daughter gently on the top of her head. "Right, Juni?" Juniper hung on her mother's legs, and they both gave Maggie a warm goodbye hug.

Emily's faith in her had been a huge relief, but Maggie still felt uneasy on her way home. What if

Juniper forgot the rule again? What if the woman in red grew bolder and tried to take her when Maggie was there? Could one young babysitter really protect her? Maggie thought back to Rebecca, the most responsible babysitter she knew. Rebecca loved baby Kyle like he was her own brother, and even she hadn't been able to keep him completely safe from the Night Queen.

And as much as Maggie hated to admit that she needed help, she knew she couldn't protect Juniper on her own. She still wasn't any braver or tougher than she was yesterday, but at least she was smart enough to know that Juniper's safety mattered a lot more than her own pride. Maggie sighed and pulled out her phone. It was time to call in her friends. She only hoped they could do a better job together than she'd been doing on her own.

CHAPTER 11

"THANKS FOR MEETING me before school." Maggie smiled gratefully at the other girls, who were gathered around a platter of doughnuts sitting on the glass counter of Kawanna's costume shop, Creature Features.

"I knew it must be something big if you were willing to get up this early," Rebecca said. She ran her fingers through her high ponytail and leaned one hip against the counter. "What's going on?"

Maggie took a nervous nibble of her pink-frosted doughnut. "I'm sorry I've been kind of avoiding everybody. It's just . . . I didn't think you guys were gonna want to hear this, so I wanted to make sure I was right before I talked about it with you," Maggie said in a rush, needing to fill the anxious, empty space with words. "I've been really stressed out about it, and I wasn't sure what to do." There. She had said it.

"Stressed about what?" Tanya asked.

Oh. Right. Maggie realized she still hadn't gotten to the point. She looked around at the girls' expectant faces. "The truth is, I'm really worried about Juniper."

Clio put her hand on Maggie's arm. "Hey, it's okay. You know you can tell us anything." She exchanged a glance with Rebecca.

Maggie shook her head and put down her doughnut. "I just wish so much that none of this happened, but it did."

"None of *what* happened?" Rebecca asked. "You still aren't making sense."

"It's just . . . I don't know. Kawanna, I know how hard you're working at the theater. I haven't said anything about what I've seen there partly because I didn't want to upset you."

Kawanna, a true night owl, was still dressed in flannel pajamas, with her red-and-blue silk bathrobe dragging on the floor behind her. She slurped a giant mug of chai. "Honey, I'm already upset from having to be awake this early. You may as well spill it."

The words came out in a rush. "I think the Twilight really is cursed. Or haunted. Or haunted *and* cursed. I don't know. Whatever it is, it's really freaking me out." Before anyone could say anything, Maggie launched into a description of what she'd seen at the Twilight, beginning with the assistant director's creepy pronouncement and ending with finding Juniper on the fire stairs.

The room was quiet. Finally, Tanya spoke. "Maggie, are you sure about this? I mean, you *kind of* think you heard something, you *kind of* think you saw something, and then you lost Juniper for a few minutes. Are you positive it's not just a combination of your imagination and new babysitter jitters? I saw how freaked out you were by that whole *Macbeth*-bad-luck thing. Sure, losing track of the kid you're watching for a few minutes is definitely stressful, but it happens sometimes if you're not careful. There doesn't need to be a supernatural reason."

"Are you kidding right now?" Maggie bristled. "When Rebecca and Clio had creepy stuff happen when they babysat, nobody thought it was because they stunk at babysitting and *imagined* it—especially when they asked for help."

"Yeah, well, you guys didn't believe us right away, either. Plus, that was different," Rebecca said.

Maggie folded her arms, eyes blazing. "You know, this is exactly why I didn't want to tell any of you. I knew it would be just like this. Of course nobody believes *me*, right? Instead you just want to throw it in my face as proof that I'm not mature or *careful* enough to handle babysitting!"

"I don't think anyone's saying that," Kawanna said gently.

"That's exactly what they're saying!" Maggie shot back.

Kawanna rubbed her forehead with both hands. "Girls, it is way too early in the morning for this," she mumbled. She took a long sip of her chai. "Can everyone just take a minute?" She closed her eyes. "Okay. Deep breath."

The four girls shifted uncomfortably. Then they each closed their eyes and took a deep breath. Maggie could feel her shoulders hunched and angry. She stretched her neck and rolled her shoulders open. She took a second deep breath. She was still mad, but she felt a little better. When she opened her eyes again, she saw the edge of a smile quirk the corner of Kawanna's mouth.

"I was really just talking to myself there, but it looks like that deep breath may have helped y'all, too," Kawanna said. "All right, now let's take a step back. I'm going to start by saying that, Maggie, I think you've been a terrific babysitter. Every time I see you at the theater, I see that Juniper is happy and her mom is happy. They obviously love you, and it's clear that Juniper feels very safe with you."

Maggie felt some of the tension ease out of her body. "Thanks," she said quietly.

Kawanna went on. "Now, I haven't seen any woman in red"—Tanya opened her mouth to interject, but Kawanna held up her hand—"but I haven't exactly been looking. I'm so busy with the play and the theater restoration that a buffalo could tap dance across the stage and I probably wouldn't notice." She yawned and took another sip of her chai. "Besides, we all know that there have been quite a few supernatural critters in Piper that children can see but adults can't."

"Okay, so Kawanna hasn't noticed anything unusual," Tanya said. "I guess that doesn't really give us any new evidence either way, then. We just have Maggie's word to go on."

"Which should be as good as Clio's or Rebecca's

word, since everyone believed *them*," Maggie said firmly.

"Hold up, hold up," Kawanna said. "Let me finish before you start biting one another's heads off. I only said I hadn't seen any woman in red. I didn't say I hadn't noticed anything unusual." Maggie couldn't help shooting Tanya a smirk of triumph.

"There have been too many accidents on set," Kawanna continued. "And Emily's dress was definitely a deliberate act. We thought it might be a jealous castmate, but everyone likes Emily, and there's no one else in the cast who auditioned for her role." She put her hand on Maggie's shoulder. "I can't offer much insight into what's happening at the theater, but I can tell you that I believe you." She looked sternly at the other three girls. "And I hope that everyone here can say the same thing." The girls nodded uncomfortably.

"Great, so apparently you'll listen to Kawanna and not me. Perfect. But since she vouched for me or whatever, maybe now can we finally start focusing on the *supernatural stuff*—like we've done when all of *you* have had problems—and less on my babysitting abilities?"

Tanya pulled at the hem of her CODE LIKE A GIRL

T-shirt. "Sorry, Mags. We didn't mean to act like we didn't think you'd be a good babysitter. It's like we all remember how nervous we were on our first babysitting jobs, and we wanted you to know that we were there to help, and I guess we just kind of went overboard. And with all this haunted curse stuff, it's just hard to imagine there could be *another* ghost in town, you know?"

"I don't see why it's so hard to believe," Maggie said. "It's not like there's only one ghost in the whole world."

"Yeah, but until recently I didn't think there were *any* ghosts, so cut me some slack," Tanya said.

"I just want to say . . . Maggie, it's not that I don't believe you. I think it's more like I don't *want* to believe you." Rebecca hugged herself. "I don't know about anyone else, but all the supernatural stuff we've been through . . . even when it's over it doesn't feel over." She chewed her thumbnail. "I have bad dreams about the Night Queen all the time."

Clio nodded slowly. "I get it. When I was baby-sitting at the Lees' I was so hoping I was wrong about all the spooky stuff in their house, because it scared me so much. But then I was also kind of mad because it felt like it took forever to convince you guys, even though it took me almost as long just to convince myself." Her eyes were earnest. "I'm really sorry if we were doing the same thing to you, Maggie."

Kawanna patted her niece's back and turned to Maggie. "So do you think the woman in red could be the Night Queen?"

"I don't know," Maggie said. "Her arms are all covered up and I can't see her face, so I don't really know what she looks like. But I don't think the Night Queen would bother hanging around a theater or ripping up Emily's dress, do you?"

"Yeah, but she would take Juniper," Rebecca answered.

"I know," Maggie said, "but I just don't think it's her. The woman in red gives me a different feeling. I bet it has something to do with the theater itself. After all, *Macbeth* is already a bad-luck play, right? And then this whole thing about the ghost light going out, too? I mean, that can't be good. I think Myles Dubois was right about the curse." She picked up her doughnut and took a bite. "What exactly is the deal with a ghost light anyway?" she asked Kawanna with her mouth full.

Kawanna put down her tea and stretched. "The ghost light is a bare bulb that's kept lit in the middle of the stage whenever the theater is dark. A lot of folks believe that theaters are full of spirits, and the ghost light keeps them happy, contented, and out of mischief. I don't know if it's true or not, but I can say that we always had ghost lights in the theaters where I worked."

Clio looked at the clock on the wall and picked up her backpack. "Well, if there is a ghost at the Twilight, we have a pretty easy way of finding out." She pulled her phone out of the outside pocket. "It's time to call in our ghost expert."

"Great idea," Maggie said. It felt good to be part of a team again, with everybody working together. Tanya and Rebecca were already making notes about how to investigate the theater, and Clio was next to them chiming in while she texted Ethan. "So, what's the plan?" Maggie asked, squeezing in. "I was thinking we could look for the ghost tonight, since there's no rehearsal. What do you guys think?" They were so busy with their conversation that they didn't look up, and Maggie felt almost as if she hadn't spoken at all.

She thought back to their conversation a few moments ago. The other girls had all apologized for doubting there was a ghost at the Twilight, but had any of them really apologized for doubting *Maggie?* Everyone seemed eager to jump in and make a plan, but it seemed strange to Maggie that nobody was asking for her ideas. After all, she was the one who had actually seen the ghost. Maggie thought she would feel relieved to have her friends by her side again, but instead she suddenly felt more alone than ever.

CHAPTER 12

LATER THAT EVENING, Ethan Underwood joined the girls on the Twilight's stage. The front of the stage was in disarray with half-painted scenery and a few plastic skeletons hung haphazardly in front of the closed curtain. For some unknown reason the taxidermic bear had been dragged out of the wings, even though Maggie was pretty sure there were no bears in *Macbeth*.

Maggie picked her way through the obstacles, and she stumbled into one of the skeletons. It startled her way more than she wanted to admit, and she smacked the bony arm in irritation. "Ugh, really?! These skeletons are seriously not helping anyone right now."

Rebecca giggled nervously. "I know, right? It's

like this place couldn't get any creepier if it tried." She leaned a wooden mallet against the wall near the front of the stage.

"Oh, trust me, it can get creepier," Maggie said. "You haven't seen the nursery yet." She watched the others setting up and tried not to wonder why she was the only one who hadn't been given anything to do.

Ethan settled cross-legged in the middle of the stage with three candles and a book on the floor in front of him. The ghost light was still out. "If the ghost light really is the problem, then why don't they just fix it or get a new one?" Tanya asked.

Clio carefully tied a bell to one of the ropes in the theater's wings. "I asked my auntie about that earlier. She said that anytime they try repairing or replacing the ghost light, sparks fly out of the outlet."

Tanya opened a purple composition book and clicked her pen. "Interesting," she said, and wrote down a few notes.

Ethan struck a match and lit the candles in front of him, and the girls joined him, sitting in a circle on the stage. Clio waited until they were all settled and then flipped off the house lights and joined them. The golden glow of the candles spilled their warm light across their anxious faces.

Maggie focused on the circle of friends around her, afraid of what she might see in the murky recesses beyond the stage. She willed herself to be brave. *It's different this time*, she told herself. *I don't have to be scared anymore, because now I'm not alone. Right?*

Ethan opened the book and ran his finger down the table of contents, talking to himself under his breath. "Are you sure you're up for this, Ethan?" Clio asked. "No offense, but things got a little out of control the last time we decided to talk to a ghost."

Ethan looked up and grinned crookedly. "Yeah, well, like I've said, I've gotten a lot better since then. Great-Grandma Moina's been helping me a lot."

"You mean your great-great-grandma Moina, who died, like, way before you were born?" Tanya asked, raising one eyebrow.

Ethan nodded. "Totally."

"Whatever you say," Tanya said. "After all, you've proved me wrong before."

Maggie picked nervously at her pink-and-black striped shoelaces. "Can we get on with it, you guys? I love this place, and I hate that it gives me the creeps now. I just want to figure out what's here and what we can do about it so things go back to normal."

Clio gave Maggie's shoulder a sympathetic squeeze. "Don't worry, we've got you covered."

Everyone quieted down, and Ethan closed his eyes. "If there are any spirits in this place, please make it known by ringing this bell," he intoned. Maggie waited breathlessly, certain the bell would ring at any moment.

Nothing happened.

"Fear not, spirits," Ethan said. "We mean you no harm. Please speak to us. We are here to help."

The bell was still. The flames on the candles burned steadily. Tanya's eyes flickered, her pen poised to record anything unusual.

"Why isn't anything happening?" Maggie whispered to Clio.

"Shh," Clio whispered back. "Ethan has to concentrate."

"Well, he needs to concentrate harder."

"Give him a minute; he's trying his best!" Clio hissed.

Maggie gave Clio the side-eye. "Just friends, huh?" Clio rolled her eyes and looked away.

Ethan swallowed audibly, and he bent over the book open in front of him, his blue-streaked bangs falling into his eyes. He flipped back and forth through the pages, seeming uncertain. "Um, I think I'm just gonna try something else. Does anyone have a flashlight?"

"I got it." Maggie slipped her phone out of her pocket and opened the flashlight app, eager to prove to the group that she could help. She held the harsh white light up at eye level, blinding the others.

Ethan shielded his eyes. "Whoa. Easy."

"Sorry." Maggie pointed the phone's light at the floor. She was glad it was too dark for the others to see her cheeks flush red with embarrassment. Even when she tried to help, it still felt like she managed to mess it up.

"I have one, too." Tanya unclipped a purple keychain flashlight from a carabiner hooked to a side loop on her jeans and clicked the button, careful to point the thin beam at the floor.

"That's perfect, T. Thanks," Rebecca said, and Maggie looked from Rebecca down at her own flashlight beam, still pointed at the floor just like Tanya's. The others turned on their phones' flashlights, and soon there was a small circle of light in the vast cavern of the darkened theater.

"Great," Ethan said. He stood up and blew out the candles. "Follow me." He led them off the stage and down into the rows of seats.

"Where are we going?" Tanya asked.

"Well," Ethan said, "I was thinking about the ghost light. The light on the stage is supposed to keep the spirits quiet, right? So maybe our lights on the stage are doing the same thing: keeping them quiet." He walked a few rows back and slid into a worn velvet seat in the middle of the row. The others followed suit.

"Okay, now, at the count of three, let's all turn off our lights. Maybe the darkness will bring our spirits back."

"Do we really have to?" Maggie's voice quivered.

"Relax, Maggie," Tanya said. "I'm sure nothing's going to happen." She sighed and put her notebook to the side. "At least I hope it doesn't, since I won't be able to record any notes. No wonder we have so little scientific evidence of the paranormal. It's pretty hard to write anything down when you can't see."

Ethan glanced along the row. "Everybody ready? Okay . . . one . . . two . . . three." Everyone clicked off their lights. The darkness felt so sudden and complete that at first Maggie saw bursts and spots of light flit across her vision, the way she did behind her eyelids when she closed her eyes against the sun. After a moment her vision adjusted, and she could make out the faint red glow of the exit signs. They looked like they were miles away.

The group sat in silence. The minutes ticked by. Maggie could hear the breathing of the others, the creaks and groans of an old building, the distant scurry of a mouse. She felt her heart beating in her chest. The cavernous theater loomed around her, and she felt small and insignificant, a tiny speck swallowed by a sea of velvet black.

Tanya shifted impatiently in the seat next to her and let out a small sigh. Finally, she spoke. "Look, Plan A and Plan B obviously aren't working. Is there a Plan C?"

Ethan cleared his throat, and his voice rose with uncertainty. "Um, not really? I guess, I don't know, maybe there isn't anything here after all?"

Just then there was a blinding flash and the stage lit up with a wide rectangle of white light. "What is it? What's happening?" Rebecca asked. Her voice was high and frightened.

Light flickered and danced across the stage. Tanya twisted and looked up behind her. "It's coming from the projection booth!" She pointed back to the stage and scrabbled under the seat for her notebook. "It looks like an old movie or something!"

Maggie squinted at the stage. Tanya was right.

Maggie could just make out a scene of women in beaded costumes and elaborate headdresses, dancing in a line. The rippling lights and shadows solidified and slipped in and out of focus as they passed across the curtain, shifting like water.

In the film a glamorous woman in a long gown stepped in front of the dancers, the image of her body perfectly superimposed over one of the plastic skeletons onstage. Her projected face flickered across the skull, shifting back and forth between beauty and horror. In the film she stood in front of the microphone and raised her arms in a gesture Maggie immediately recognized. She tapped Clio's arm next to her. "Guys, I think that's our ghost! The lady in the film has got to be the woman in red! She's here! What does she want?"

Ethan's voice sounded faint and confused. "I . . . I don't know."

"What are you talking about?" Maggie demanded. "Obviously the ghost is trying to tell us something. So, talk to her!"

"I've been trying," Ethan said. "But there isn't any spirit here that's communicating with me."

"Well, what do you call that?" She pointed at the stage. "I'd say that's some pretty clear communication, wouldn't you?"

Ethan shook his head. "Sure, but the problem is I don't know what's doing it." His voice was emphatic. "I don't feel any spiritual presence at all!"

"I don't get it," Maggie said in frustration.

The projector stopped and the stage went black again. There was no sound in the darkness except for Ethan's quiet answer.

"I don't know what the woman in red is, but she definitely isn't a ghost."

CHAPTER 13

EVERYONE SAT IN silence for a moment as Ethan's words sunk in. Finally, Clio spoke. "What do you mean?"

Ethan turned on his flashlight and stood up. "I mean that whatever supernatural entity is here, it's not something I know how to communicate with."

"Well, can't you try?" Maggie turned on her own flashlight and stood up, too.

Ethan shrugged helplessly. "Sorry, Maggie, but I'm strictly a ghost guy. Asking me to communicate with something else is like asking a Mandarin speaker to suddenly turn around and translate Spanish. I can't do it."

"Yeah, but what about animals? You can communicate with them!" Maggie said.

Ethan sighed. "Yeah, okay, fine. Then I can confidently tell you that the woman in red is not an animal, either."

"I know that," Maggie said, exasperated, "but the point is if you can communicate with both of those, maybe you can do more. Maybe you have hidden talents you don't even know about still."

"Don't push it, Maggie," Clio said. "If he says he can't do it, he can't do it." She stood up and started walking down the row toward the lobby with the others close behind her. "I'm going to text my auntie to come pick us up."

Maggie trailed behind. "Wait, so we're just gonna give up? What about Emily? What about Juniper?"

Clio flicked on the house lights. "Nobody's saying anything about giving up. We just need to hold a beat and think about what we know before we do anything else." She paused and looked around at the others, dropping her voice. "But since we don't know exactly what we're dealing with or how dangerous she is, maybe we should get out of here first." Clio led them through the lobby and out the front door, where they stood shivering under the awning. She turned to lock the padlock on the door. "Don't worry, Mags," she said. "We're your friends, okay? We got this."

Tanya flipped the collar up on her long coat and absentmindedly spiked her short hair. "Okay. I think we can agree at this point that there's something supernatural in there." The others nodded. "And it's obviously not a ghost or a changeling, and it's probably not the Night Queen. So our next step is to find out what it is."

"Looks like it's research time again." Clio rubbed her hands together. "Who's up for a visit to the library tomorrow after school?"

Maggie made a gagging face. "No way! I'm not getting stuck behind one of those boring microfilm machines again."

"But I thought you were the one who's so gung ho to get to the bottom of this," Clio said. "And to do that we've *all* got to be willing to put in the work."

"I know that," Maggie snapped. "And I've done just as much work as you have! But this time I have a better idea." She turned to Tanya. "If we borrowed some of the equipment from the projector room upstairs, do you think you could get it to work?"

Tanya nodded. "For sure, but what are we going to do with it? We could watch that film clip a million times and still not get any closer to figuring out who the woman is."

"You're right," Maggie said. "But I think I know someone who could."

. . . . .

On Saturday morning Kawanna helped Maggie and Tanya unload the film reel and a small, portable projector in front of an old, Spanish-style apartment building with a neglected, algae-coated fountain in the courtyard.

"Are you sure you girls will be okay?" Kawanna asked. "Do you want me to come in with you?"

Maggie did, but she shook her head. "We're good, but thanks so much for the ride." Myles Dubois was already high-strung enough, and now that Clio's aunt had taken over his position of assistant director for *Macbeth*, Maggie wasn't sure he would welcome seeing Kawanna at his door.

As Maggie and Tanya crossed the courtyard, Maggie lowered her voice. "I just want to make sure we have our story straight. We're doing a research project for school on the Twilight Theater, and we found this film in the projector booth, right?"

Tanya lugged the projector by its handle. "Yep, and we're hoping to interview him for the oral history part of the project." She pulled open the door, and they walked into the building's threadbare lobby. They passed a few sagging leather armchairs and an empty reception desk that probably once held a concierge in the building's glory days.

Maggie couldn't find any buzzer, but near the mailboxes there was a list of tenants and their apartment numbers. Myles Dubois was on the top floor, in Apartment 13. "It figures," Tanya grumbled, heaving the projector along the chipped marble floor.

"Don't worry, there's an elevator." Maggie helped Tanya drag the projector into the rickety old elevator and pressed the button. "I really hope he doesn't kick us out."

"Would he do that?" Tanya asked.

"I don't know, maybe," Maggie said. "I've never really talked to him."

The bell for the floor dinged and the elevator doors slid open. "Wait a minute, I thought you knew this person."

Maggie and Tanya stood in front of Apartment 13. "Not exactly, but I know *of* him." Maggie rang the doorbell. "Whatever, I'm sure it will go fine."

When the door to Apartment 13 opened a few moments later, it was anything but fine. "What is the meaning of this intrusion?" Myles Dubois's resonant voice boomed through the empty hallway. He stood in the doorway with his arms folded and his chin lowered, his gaunt face glowering down at them over his tortoiseshell glasses. He wore linty black trousers and a black turtleneck sweater with the cuff of one sleeve partially unraveled. A black beret was perched on his head, and his snow-white hair puffed out beneath it.

Tanya cleared her throat. "We're doing a history project for school, and we need to interview you."

"This isn't amateur hour, young lady. If you want to conduct an interview, you'll have to go through my agent," he snapped.

"Oh, okay. Sorry," Tanya said. "Who's your agent?"

"I don't have one!" he shouted, and slammed the door in the girls' faces.

Maggie and Tanya looked at each other. "Well, that went well," Tanya said. She started lugging the projector back toward the elevator.

"Wait," Maggie said. "We're not going to give up that easily."

"Yeah, we are, Mags. He slammed the door in our faces."

"I think there might be a better way to convince him to help us."

"What was wrong with the way I did it? I stuck to the story, didn't I? I think I was very clear."

"Nothing's wrong with what you did. Just let me try one more time, okay?"

Tanya sighed. "Fine."

Maggie rang the bell again and braced herself. The door opened a crack. Myles Dubois's wild white eyebrows sank down over his eyes, the long hairs poking forward like antennae. Before he could say anything, Maggie spoke. "Please, Mr. Dubois. Please just hear me out before you close the door again."

The door stayed open, so Maggie went on. "Everyone in town says you were one of the greatest actors that Piper has ever seen." The eyebrows rose slightly, and the harsh lines around the mouth softened. Maybe it was working. She pointed to Tanya. "We found an old film of a stage show. We've only seen a tiny clip of it, but we think there's a good chance that you might be in it." Maggie was pretty sure the film was way too old for there to be any chance of Mr. Dubois being in it, but he didn't have to know that. "And honestly, sir . . ." Maggie watched his eyes, wondering if she had pushed too hard with the *sir*. ". . . since nobody knows more about theater than you do, we would love to hear some of your favorite stories about your *enormous* contributions to American theater." She was laying it on really thick.

Mr. Dubois preened. "Well, why didn't you mention that in the first place? I'm always happy to talk with fans." He swept the door open wide and welcomed them in.

The apartment walls were covered in posters, playbills, and framed photos of Mr. Dubois. Maggie looked closer. They were autographed. *What kind of person hangs up autographed photos of himself in his own home?* Maggie wondered. *Probably the same kind of person who would believe that a couple of twelve-year-olds are his biggest fans.* There was a glass cabinet with some statuettes and awards in it. They weren't any that Maggie recognized, but they were spotless, as though he kept them regularly cleaned and polished.

A large home-movie screen covered one wall, and there was an old-fashioned film projector set up in the middle of the room. Tanya looked down at the projector she was carrying and then back at Maggie. *Sorry,* Maggie mouthed.

Tanya brought out the film canister and attached the spool onto the projector, threading the thin film strip through the narrow grooves and hooking it into place. She turned on the projector, and

Mr. Dubois closed the heavy blackout curtains at the windows.

There were a few flashes of shapes and numbers, and then the silent line of dancing ladies appeared on the screen. Tanya adjusted the focus until it was clear. There were the sparkly outfits and elaborate beaded headdresses. It reminded Maggie of the time her parents took her to see the Radio City holiday show in New York. "Are those the Rockettes?" she asked.

Myles stroked his goatee. "The Rockettes started in 1925, so it could be, but I don't think so. This looks like the Ziegfeld Follies, judging by the costumes."

"What's that?" Maggie asked.

"They were Broadway shows similar to the vaudeville revues that were popular at the time. Both shows were mixes of acts highlighting some of the most popular singers and comedians of the day, but the Follies always featured the legendary Ziegfeld girl chorus lines. Many starlets owed their early careers to the master producer Florenz Ziegfeld, Jr."

On-screen the woman took her place in front of the microphone. Her hair was platinum blond and framed her face in close-cropped waves. She wore a glittering gown, and her lashes were so long they cast shadows on her cheeks when she closed her eyes and began to sing. "I don't believe it," Mr. Dubois said, gripping the arms of his chair.

"What is it?" Maggie asked. Tanya pulled out her notebook, her mechanical pencil poised over a clean page.

"This recording you found is very rare! If I'm not mistaken, that's Vivien Vane! She got her start as a Ziegfeld chorus girl, where it seemed she would languish forever in obscurity, but she shot to overnight stardom when one of the lead acts failed to show one day and she stepped in and took her place. She became one of the most sought-after starlets in the vaudeville circuit. She had been poised to make a splash in legitimate theater and perhaps even Hollywood, but unfortunately, she never did make the transition to international stardom."

"Why not?" Tanya asked.

"Well, she was scheduled to play Lady Macbeth at the grand opening of the Twilight Theater right here in Piper. She was seen arriving at the theater on opening night, but she didn't appear onstage for her cue, and an understudy had to step in."

"Why didn't she go on?" Maggie asked. She couldn't imagine giving up a chance to appear onstage in front of a crowd of admirers.

"Nobody knows," Mr. Dubois answered.

"What do you mean?" Tanya asked. "Didn't someone ask her?"

"They couldn't. After that night she was never seen again."

CHAPTER 14

MAGGIE TRIED TO keep her face composed, but her insides were hopping around like popcorn. Could Vivien Vane be the woman in red?

The actor went on. "The Twilight's opening was meant to be one of the greatest in theater history. It was sold out, and Graham Reynard Faust, the owner, spared no expense to produce a show that would make the whole country take notice. He had personally booked Vivien Vane to play Lady Macbeth in the performance. It was a perfect opportunity for both of them. Vane would reach the next level of stardom, and Faust dreamed of all the money that would come rolling in. But alas, it was not to be."

"What happened?" Maggie asked, her voice hushed.

"It was such a perfect storm of bad luck that the theater has never recovered from the curse of that night."

Tanya snorted derisively, startling Maggie. She had been so absorbed in the actor's story that she had forgotten Tanya was in the room. "Don't tell me you believe in curses, too," Tanya said, rolling her eyes. Maggie tried to give her a *knock it off* glare, but Tanya ignored her. "I mean, it's a ridiculous idea!"

Mr. Dubois turned off the projector. "I beg your pardon, young lady, but what on earth could you possibly know about it? Why, look at you. You can't be older than seven." Tanya looked affronted, and Maggie bit her lip, trying not to snicker. Mr. Dubois obviously hadn't spent much time around kids.

He stood up and opened the curtains before pulling a heavy maroon scrapbook out of a carved black bookshelf along the wall. He lay it open on the glass-topped coffee table in front of the sofa and turned it to face the two girls.

First was a front-page clipping from the *Register*, dated October 24, 1929. The image showed the Twilight's marquee all gleaming and new, with a red carpet rolled out in front of it. TWILIGHT THEATER PREPARES FOR HISTORIC OPENING, the headline declared. Maggie skimmed the article, a glowing piece about the huge success the performance was likely to bring to Faust, the actors, and the entire town. "Jeez," Maggie said. "Did this Faust guy own the paper or something?"

Mr. Dubois arched one eyebrow. "Very perceptive, young lady. Faust didn't own the paper, but his brother-in-law did. In fact, the *Register*'s owner was one of the theater's major investors. Which may explain this." He turned the page. The next headline was dated October 25, 1929: THEATER OPENING AN UNMITIGATED DISASTER.

Tanya bent forward and started reading aloud. "Okay, so when Vivien Vane didn't show up, her understudy, Norma Desmond, took her place. But it says here that Norma did a good job." She looked up. "What was the problem?"

"Keep reading," Mr. Dubois commanded.

Tanya's eyes went back to the page. "Oh . . . oh! Wow. Okay."

"What does it say?" Maggie demanded.

"Halfway through the play all the cigarette smoke from the audience set off the brand-new, state-of-the-art sprinkler system, drenching the stage and the guests. It shorted out the electrical system, and the entire theater went dark. There was a panic, and a few people were trampled in the push for the exits."

She looked up at Maggie. "But nobody was killed. Just minor injuries." She looked back down at the clipping. "They had to refund everyone's tickets and close the theater for repairs. It was a huge loss."

"But that's not all." Mr. Dubois turned the page. The dateline of the next article was also October 25, 1929, but the headline was much larger, the heavy black letters spanning the page: WORST STOCK MARKET CRASH IN HISTORY.

It didn't mean anything to Maggie, but Tanya's eyes were wide. "This was the start of the Great Depression, right?"

Myles nodded. "Both Faust and his brother-in-law had leveraged all their stock holdings to build the theater. When the market crashed, they lost everything. After their ill-fated opening night, the theater was never able to reopen."

Maggie's jaw dropped. *"Never?"*

"The Great Depression and the war kept it shuttered through the forties. In the 1950s there was a resurgence of interest in old movie palaces, and various entrepreneurs tried to reopen the Twilight, but every effort ended in failure. Not one single production ever lasted more than one night."

Tanya blinked. "Wait. Not even one? How is

that possible? The mathematical odds against that happening are enormous."

Mr. Dubois gave an elegant shrug. "Curses don't care about math." He flipped through page after page of the scrapbook, and Maggie watched the headlines flash by. MOVIE FLOP CLOSES AFTER ONE DAY (1957). MAGIC SHOW MISHAP HORRIFIES AUDIENCE (1970). CONCERT CUT SHORT WHEN POP STAR'S HAIR CATCHES FIRE (1983). The list went on. Tanya pulled out her camera and snapped photos of the headline pages.

"So the curse is real," Maggie breathed. She shot a triumphant look at Tanya and noticed that familiar expression of grudging acceptance on her friend's face.

"Well, there obviously must be some reason I have turned down every invitation to perform at the Twilight. As sought-after a performer as I am, you can imagine what a sacrifice this was for me."

Maggie looked around the ramshackle apartment, with its yellowed posters and out-of-date furniture. It didn't look like many people were beating down his door. "Why did you agree to work with the new theater company, then?"

Mr. Dubois sighed heavily. "I was offered the part of Macbeth first, you know." Maggie nodded along, but she doubted it. He was about forty years too old to play the lead.

He sat up straighter and put his hand to his heart. "'Alas,' I said to the director, 'Irene, you know I can't possibly set foot on the Twilight stage as a performer. Please stop begging me!' But she wouldn't relent, so I finally agreed to act as the assistant director as a favor to her. I was foolish and naive enough to think that perhaps I could avoid the theater's curse, but once I saw the ghost light was extinguished . . ." He sighed dramatically. "I knew the production was doomed. I had no choice but to bow out gracefully." Maggie almost laughed out loud. His exit had been anything but graceful.

Tanya looked down at the notes she had been taking. "Where do you think this curse came from? I mean, what do you think would cause it?"

Mr. Dubois took a deep breath and closed his eyes, thinking. "I can think of only one reason."

"What is it?" Tanya asked.

But Maggie figured out the answer before he even spoke. She understood the hunger for fame, and she knew that there was nothing on earth that could make an actress willingly walk away from a chance at stardom. Maggie couldn't begin to guess what had transpired on that ill-fated opening night, but she did know one thing: Something terrible had happened to Vivien Vane, and the curse was her revenge.

CHAPTER 15

LATER THAT NIGHT Kawanna handed Clio a set of keys and put her hands gently on her niece's head. "Explore all you want, but at least promise me that you'll be careful." She had more lines around her eyes than Maggie remembered, and a few gray hairs had begun to thread their way through her dreadlocks, but Maggie was relieved to see that her nails were freshly painted red, with a tiny silver knife on each nail.

"We will," Maggie promised. She pointed at Kawanna's hands. "I love them!"

Kawanna waggled her fingers. "Bloody daggers! Getting ready for opening night next week!" She gave a last wave to the girls and swept back through the double doors to the auditorium.

"Where's Juniper?" Rebecca asked. The girls sat on the landing of the grand staircase in the Twilight's lobby with a theater blueprint spread out on the floor in front of them.

"They're not working on any of Emily's scenes, so she didn't have to be at rehearsal," Maggie said. "The rest of the cast is in there." She pointed to the closed sets of double doors leading to the auditorium. "And hopefully, that's where all the spooky stuff will stay tonight."

"So we have the rest of the theater to ourselves to explore?" Clio asked. She stood up to examine the multitiered dry crystal fountain on the landing. Her finger brushed a line of dust off the gold basin, and she wiped her hand on her jeans, careful to avoid the embroidered flowers that twined up one leg.

"Hey, don't forget we're not here for fun," Maggie said.

"'*Not here for fun*'?" Rebecca folded her arms and narrowed her eyes. "All right, who are you and what did you do with the real Maggie?" she joked.

"You guys, I'm serious. We have to find out what cursed the Twilight. Mr. Dubois said it must be revenge for something, and it's definitely connected to Vivien Vane. I think Vivien is targeting Emily because she's playing the role that Vivien was meant to play—Lady Macbeth. We have to protect Emily and Juniper, and maybe by figuring out what happened to Vivien, we can find a way to break the curse before it's too late."

"But I don't understand how she can still be alive," Rebecca said. "I mean, she'd be like way over a hundred years old by now!" She squatted over the blueprint, the loaded pockets of her fitted black cargo pants straining with the gear she had packed for a night of urban exploring. Instead of her signature stylish high-tops, she wore an old pair of classic black vans with holes in the toes.

"Well, according to Ethan she's definitely not dead," Clio said, dusting off the hem of her blush-pink linen top. "I wish he were here tonight, too. He wanted to come, but his family's heading out of town early tomorrow morning, and he had to pack."

"Where are they going?" Rebecca asked.

"His mom finished her PhD, so their family is celebrating with a trip to Maui," Clio answered. "They won't be back until after opening night."

"Bummer," Maggie said. "Even though Vivien's not a ghost, it would be nice to have him around to help anyway."

Tanya tapped the blueprint with one finger. "We

may not know what Vivien is, but we do know that she walked into the Twilight on opening night and was never seen again. Somewhere in this theater there must be a clue about what happened to her. All we have to do is find it."

"But this place is huge," Clio said. "Where do we start?"

"I was thinking about that," Maggie said. "Remember when I found Juniper on the stairwell headed down to the basement? There must be something down there. And this time I came prepared." She pulled a glittery pink headlamp out of her new silver, quilted backpack and put it on. It matched perfectly with her black PART UNICORN T-shirt and pink and black star-print leggings.

"Very stylish," Tanya said drily. She strapped on a simple black headlamp and clipped an extra flashlight to the belt of her boyfriend jeans. She slipped a small hiking backpack over the shoulders of her FEMINIST T-shirt and stood up. "All right, Mags, show us where to go."

Maggie stood up straighter. *Finally. A chance to be in charge.* The others followed Maggie down the stairs. She paused in front of the dark doorway to the nursery.

"What's in there?" Clio whispered.

"That's the creepy nursery," Maggie whispered back.

"Should we check it out?" Clio asked.

Maggie shuddered. "Not if we don't have to." She pushed open the fire door and flipped on the basement stairwell lights. The bare bulbs were sparsely placed, and several were burnt out, so the way downward was shadowy and treacherous, occasional pools of yellow light beckoning like oases. Maggie pointed down to the first landing. "That's where I found Juniper last time." She gripped the painted metal handrail tightly and started down the staircase, her friends following closely behind.

They reached the landing and stopped. The flight of stairs below them was unlit. Maggie looked into the inky darkness with trepidation. What was waiting for them down there? She felt frozen in place.

"Okay, everybody. Headlamps on." Tanya switched on her own and patted Maggie on the shoulder. "You still leading the way?"

"Um, yeah. Sure." Maggie gulped and tried to pry her fingers from the handrail, but she couldn't seem to make herself let go.

Clio looked at Maggie's anxious expression. "Actually, why don't we let Tanya go first?"

Maggie turned to look at Clio. "Why?"

"She and her family go camping and hiking all the time. You know how good she is at that outdoorsy stuff."

"But we're not outdoors," Maggie said.

"You know what I mean. That walking-around-in-the-dark kind of stuff."

Maggie bristled. "And I'm not?"

"I don't know; I'm sure you're great at it, too. You can go first if you want to."

Maggie didn't want to go first. *At all*. She considered both the outdoors and the dark to be hazardous environments she should avoid at all costs. Both created too many opportunities to walk face-first into a spiderweb. "It's okay. Tanya can take the lead. Just this once."

"I'll go last and make sure nobody falls behind," Rebecca offered. The group slowly made their way down the second staircase until they reached the bottom. Tanya played her flashlight beam over an arched tunnel that branched in several directions. The walls and ceiling were made of stone and seemed to be much older than the rest of the theater.

"It's like a labyrinth down here," Rebecca said. "Which way do we go?"

"Good question," Tanya said. "Should we split up?"

"Are you kidding?! No way!" Maggie grabbed Tanya's arm. "We could get lost down here, or worse! Besides, we still don't know where Vivien is. We have to stick together."

Tanya sighed. "Fine." She pointed to the tunnel's main branch. "Let's go that way." They followed it, pausing to point their flashlights into the arched doorways they passed. The first few looked like storage rooms, with old cartons of stage lights, stacks of colored gels, and snaky piles of orange extension cords. As the tunnel moved downward, the chambers along it were empty. Tanya was moving quickly now, but she stopped abruptly.

"What is it?" Maggie asked.

"Look." Tanya's headlamp reflected off a pool of water that stretched as far as the light could reach. "The river must have flooded this part of the tunnel. Let's turn back and try another one."

This time they followed the route that branched to the left. The storage rooms along this route held an odder assortment of items. In one Maggie noticed a purple-and-black box with slots in it, the kind a magician would use to saw someone in half. She noticed a large rusty stain at the bottom of the box, near one of the sawing slots. She remembered the *Register*'s headline about the ill-fated magic show, and her stomach twisted. "We should keep going."

The final storage room at the tunnel's end was different. Instead of an open archway it had a heavy metal door with a rusted iron padlock. "Why does this one have a door?" Clio asked, tugging on the padlock.

"Probably to keep people from finding whatever's inside." Tanya reached into her backpack and pulled out a small J-shaped crowbar. "Which is why I brought this." She threaded the notched end of the crowbar into the lock's loop and pulled on the handle, straining against the lock until it snapped open.

"Whoa," Maggie said. "I was totally about to make fun of you for bringing a crowbar, but never mind."

"Never underestimate the power of physics," Tanya said with a grin. She dropped the crowbar back into her pack and gently pulled open the door.

The beams of their flashlights revealed a small chamber with a stone floor, covered by a threadbare Persian rug. There was a long, narrow table near the doorway with a tarnished silver candelabra in the middle. Mountains of candle wax covered the table's surface. Clio picked up a book of matches sitting on the table's edge. Maggie could see a green horseshoe and the words GOOD LUCK CLUB printed in red on the matchbook's cover. Clio lit the pale-pink candles, revealing more of the chamber.

A sagging red and gold brocade divan was pushed against one wall, a pile of stained silk pillows clustered along one end. A vanity with an angled gold mirror and a torn red velvet stool took up the opposite wall. Maggie could see pasty stage makeup laid out in front of the mirror, and one of those old-fashioned cut-glass perfume bottles. There was a wheeled clothing rack shoved in next to it with moth-eaten fur coats and velvet capes draped haphazardly on the old satin hangers. Waxy red tally marks covered every wall from ceiling to floor. Curled, yellowed posters for the Ziegfeld Follies and other old shows hung like peeling skin, and mummified bouquets of roses, dried and black, sat in vases on every available surface. In one corner of the room the wall had begun to crumble, leaving a dark hole behind. "What is this place?" Rebecca whispered.

"It looks like a dressing room," Clio said. She picked up one of the cards tucked into the vanity's mirror and read it aloud. *"To Vivien: Best wishes for a dazzling opening night. Cecil B. DeMille."* She put the card down, puzzled. "Why was Vivien's dressing room all the way down here?" She looked again at the door. "And why was it locked from the outside?"

Clio noticed another note, this one fastened to the wall with the tip of a knife. She pried the knife out of the wall and read the note: *"Vivien—I'm sorry. It's my only chance to shine. —Norma."* She looked up. "Norma Desmond was her understudy, and it's dated October 24, 1929, the opening night of the Twilight."

Just then, the door swung shut with a clang. Rebecca jumped back, and her headlamp revealed deep scratches in the door's surface.

Her eyes widened with fear. "This wasn't Vivien's dressing room. It was her prison."

CHAPTER
16

"*VIVIEN'S UNDERSTUDY LOCKED* her in this room on opening night, and she never came back for her?" Maggie gasped. "How long do you think she was trapped down here?"

Rebecca pointed at the walls of endless lipstick-red tally marks, and Maggie swallowed thickly. "We should go back upstairs."

Rebecca pushed the door, but it didn't budge. The girls looked at one another. "There's no way this door can be locked—we broke off the padlock. It must just be stuck." Rebecca grabbed the handle and shook it violently. Nothing happened.

"Or maybe Vivien locked us in," Maggie said anxiously. "Clio, does your aunt know we're down here?"

Clio grimaced. "She knows we're at the theater, but that's about it. I'll text her." She pulled out her phone and swore under her breath. "No signal. Of course!" Clio tapped futilely at the home screen.

Maggie fought a rising panic. "How are we gonna get out of here?" She opened the vanity drawers and started rummaging through them.

"What are you looking for?" Rebecca asked.

"I don't know!" A lipstick tube bounced out of a drawer and rolled along the floor. Maggie turned to the clothing rack, shoving aside the fur and capes.

Rebecca shouted and pounded on the door.

Tanya raised her voice above the panic in the room. "Guys, just chill for a second." But nobody was listening. Finally, she put two fingers in her mouth and let out a piercing whistle. Everyone stopped and stared at her.

"I didn't know people could really whistle like that in real life," Maggie whispered, stunned. "I thought it was just on TV."

"Yeah, well, it took a lot of practice," Tanya said. "Now, look, don't take this the wrong way, but if and when the Zombie Apocalypse comes, I definitely don't want to be stuck with any of you. We've been in this room for less than five minutes, and you're already panicking." She pointed to a corner of the room. "In case you hadn't noticed, there's a huge hole in the wall."

"Oh. Right." Clio looked sheepish. "But how do you know it leads anywhere?"

Tanya shined her flashlight into the cavity. It opened into a pipe-filled tunnel. "Vivien obviously must have gotten out of here somehow."

"No thanks to Norma Desmond," Maggie said. "I can't believe she locked Vivien down here and never came back for her!" She bent down and began tidying up the evidence of her frantic search, putting everything back into the vanity drawers. She picked up an old news clipping that showed a fresh-faced Vivien, eyes shining with excitement, posing in front of the Twilight's marquee. MISS VANE "HONORED AND THRILLED" TO MAKE STAGE DEBUT AS LADY MACBETH, the headline read. The article went on to detail the time and work the actress had put into the role, and it ended with a quote from Vivien that made Maggie's breath catch in her throat: *I've been dreaming of this moment ever since I was a little girl.* Maggie shook her head angrily. "I don't care how much Norma wanted her chance to 'shine.' I think what she did was unforgivable."

"Remember, opening night was a total disaster, and the theater closed the next day," Tanya replied. "I don't think Norma left her here on purpose."

"Like that makes it any better?" Maggie asked. "What an awful way to die."

"Or not die," Rebecca said, touching the red lines that marked the days Vivien had spent trapped and alone.

"But if she can't still be alive and she isn't dead, then what is she?" Clio asked. "And how did she end up this way?"

Maggie smoothed the clothing rack. "I think she's kind of like . . . a ghoul. She was supposed to die, but something trapped her spirit inside her body and kept her here. I just wish we knew what." She pushed some satin hangers aside to make room, revealing a nook in the stone wall behind.

"What's that?" Tanya asked. She helped Maggie roll the rack out of the way to get a closer look. The nook was piled with dead flowers, melted candles, and torn shreds of fabric and leather that were arranged like offerings.

Maggie recognized the strips of black crocodile-print leather and heavy red velvet immediately, and she was pretty sure she knew where the fluffy white faux fur came from. "I think these are Emily's missing things," she said, holding up the strips.

"That's disturbing," Rebecca said. She looked closer. "What is this, some kind of creepy shrine?" She shined the beam of her flashlight over a tile mosaic that covered the back wall of the nook. It showed a clearing with red-leaved trees arching over an outdoor stage. There was a white throne in the center with a figure on it, but the features were obscured by a fistful of dead roses and daisies leaning against the wall. Rebecca pushed the flowers aside and leaned in for a closer look. Suddenly she jumped back with a gasp and dropped her flashlight like it was on fire.

"What's wrong?!" Maggie cried. Rebecca pointed wordlessly. The figure on the throne had a long dress and a silver ram's-horn crown. Her blue skin glinted with diamond-chip stars. Instead of hair, jointed brown spider's legs pointed out from her head at odd angles. It was the Night Queen.

"Oh, please, no. Not again," Maggie said, shaking her head. "What is this doing here?"

"What do you think?" Clio asked hollowly. "The Night Queen is behind this somehow. She has to be."

"Hey, we don't know that for sure," Tanya said

encouragingly, but her voice lacked conviction. "Maybe it's just a coincidence. Maybe it's just . . . um . . . a really cool piece of art. You know, hidden all the way down in this . . . basement." The others just stared at her. "Okay, yeah, no, the Night Queen is definitely involved. It doesn't take a rocket science degree to make that connection."

"So not only do we have to figure out how to protect Emily—and the whole theater—from this stupid curse, but now we have to worry about the Night Queen again, too?" Maggie said. "Oh, that's just perfect." She closed her eyes and took a deep breath. She still had nightmares about their previous run-ins with the undead queen. Maggie would awaken in a cold sweat, certain she could feel the grip of rotten hands dragging her down. And as brave a face as the other girls had tried to put on, now she knew they still had nightmares, too.

"Let's get out of here," Clio said quietly. She clicked on her headlamp and led the others through the hole in the wall. They followed the pipes where they led back to the main tunnel and the staircase. No one spoke as they made their way down the spartan hallway and back into the frayed elegance of the Twilight's lower levels. The details of the old theater began to take on new meaning as the girls passed through the empty rooms; the Night Queen's touch seemed to be everywhere they looked. Rebecca pointed wordlessly at the inlaid wooden owls on the double doors that led to the cocktail bar. And the carpeting beneath their feet: Was that a pattern of intertwined maple leaves?

As they walked back upstairs Maggie found she no longer cared if her friends still doubted her. The enormity of what they faced descended like a heavy weight upon her shoulders, blocking out everything else. Learning the identity of the woman in red had made everything seem way less scary for a while, and Maggie had started to feel a kind of pity for Vivien and the awful events that had led to the Twilight's curse. But now that she realized the Night Queen was involved, Maggie felt only fear again. If the girls couldn't break the Night Queen's hold over Vivien, then everyone at the theater was in serious danger, especially Emily.

CHAPTER
17

THE GIRLS MET at Creature Features on Sunday morning, where their usual platter of doughnuts was waiting on the counter, along with a pot of Kawanna's famous jasmine tea. The theater's blueprints were rolled out on the floor, and a stack of old books sat on the Persian carpet nearby.

Never one for punctuality, Maggie was the last to arrive, and the other girls were already leafing through a few open books on the counter while they nibbled their breakfast. It was late enough in the morning that Kawanna wasn't wearing her usual morning meeting robe and slippers. Instead she had on a pair of boyfriend jeans with a white linen tee and a silver and turquoise squash-blossom necklace. Her hair was twisted up in an orange-and-turquoise print headwrap. She had dark circles under her eyes, but she gave Maggie a bright smile.

Maggie plucked her favorite pink-frosted doughnut from the tarnished silver platter and took a huge bite before resting it on one of Kawanna's spiderweb-patterned cloth napkins. "Please tell me you've already come up with a plan," Maggie said half-jokingly.

Tanya grinned and shook her head. "I wish. But Clio and Kawanna did find something that might be able to help us."

Clio looked up from the book she was reading. "Do you know the legend of Theophilus of Adana?"

"Seriously?" Maggie looked at her. "Why are you even asking?"

"Okay, well, you never know." Clio twisted her silver ring around her finger, choosing her words carefully. "In it this priest, Theophilus, makes a deal with the devil: his soul in exchange for a job he really wanted."

"He sold his soul for a *job*? That is truly pathetic."

"Anyway, it's the earliest known legend of a person making a supernatural deal with their soul. And since then there have been tons of stories, plays, and movies about that idea. And at least a few rumors about real people doing it, too, like this old blues musician, Robert Johnson. People said he couldn't play guitar, like, at all, and then one day he was suddenly amazing at it."

"Okay," Maggie said. "So where does the Night Queen fit in?"

"Well, last night my auntie and I started doing a bunch more research on the theater's history. Remember that guy, Graham Reynard Faust, the one who built the theater?"

"Yeah," Maggie said. "He was that rich guy who lost all his money."

"Sure, but he didn't *start out* rich," Clio said. "When he first showed up in Piper he didn't have a penny to his name, and nobody had ever heard of him. But then he disappeared for a little while, and when he came back he suddenly had all this money and plans to build the theater. Nobody could ever figure out where the money came from." She searched through a pile of papers and pulled one out. "And some people said he cut a lot of corners to build the Twilight in record time. There were some accidents during construction, and a few of the workers were never heard from again. Some folks in town wanted to open an investigation, but nothing came of it. It was like all of a sudden, nobody could touch him."

Rebecca grabbed Maggie's arm and pulled her

over to the blueprints on the floor. "Okay, now, close your eyes for a second and think. Describe the curtains on the Twilight's stage."

Maggie thought for a moment. "Midnight blue . . . with silver stars." She opened her eyes and saw Rebecca's brown eyes sparkling back.

"And last night we all noticed the owls on the doors to the bar, and the maple leaf pattern on the carpet, right?"

"Right."

"That wasn't just a coincidence. There are more owls and maple leaves in the fancy carving around the stage." She pointed to a plan drawing of the grand staircase. "And look at this sketch of the grillwork on the staircase. Ram's horns."

"Once you know to look for it, it's everywhere," Tanya continued. "The Stardust Ballroom had the ceiling painted to look like the night sky. The old restaurant was called the Moonlight Serenade."

"So what are you saying?" Maggie asked. "Do you think this Graham guy made some sort of deal with the Night Queen, and then came back and built this whole theater for her?"

"Uh-huh." Clio pushed up the sleeves of her fox-print shirtdress and picked up a chocolate-frosted doughnut. "And it's not the first time it's happened in town. Aunt Kawanna and I were looking through Miss Pearl's papers again last night—"

"Is that the name of the lady who used to own your shop?" Maggie asked.

Kawanna nodded. "There were several other stories in the town's history of people who disappeared for a while and came back with unexplained money or talents." She folded her arms and raised one eyebrow. "One of them was a clockmaker—"

Maggie's eyes widened. "OMG, the clock we found at the old Plunkett mansion! I'm so glad we got rid of that thing!"

"Exactly! And we think the theater might have been built with some kind of similar purpose. Listen to this," Clio said. She opened to a marked page in a slim, red leather-bound volume and read aloud:

> They build a temple to the Queene
> Upon its walls her marks be seen
> The icy light of fullest moon
> Then opens up the mortals' doom
> And power faint becomes a flood
> With sacrifice, a toll of blood.

"Whatever that means, it sounds really bad," Maggie said. "Doom? Blood? Sacrifice?"

"I know," Tanya said. "The poem suggests that the theater was supposed to become some kind of power center for the Night Queen. *'Power faint becomes a flood.'* Not only would it allow her to come into our world whenever she wanted, but it would also let her stay here."

"No!" Maggie cried.

"Lucky for us, it doesn't seem to have worked right. Or at least, not yet. Clio thinks something might have gone wrong the night the theater opened," Rebecca said.

"Are you kidding?" Maggie grabbed another doughnut. "*Everything* went wrong that night!"

"Yeah, but it's possible that something went wrong for the Night Queen, too," Clio answered. "Faust intentionally planned the opening night of the theater for a full moon. Because according to the poem, in order to harness the kind of power the Night Queen needed to make the theater hers forever, there needed to be . . . um . . . a . . . *sacrifice* during the full moon."

Maggie stared at Clio, speechless. Finally she found her voice. "And this Faust guy was totally okay with that?" She felt sick.

Tanya sighed. "Maybe he didn't know." She opened her laptop and pulled up photos she had taken of the headlines from Mr. Dubois's scrap-book. "I think the Night Queen didn't plan for Vivien's understudy just to lock her up for a few hours. I think she expected Norma to do something more, um, permanent. And when she didn't, the queen was hoping that the other accidents that night would give her what she wanted. But no one died, and she lost her chance."

"But then why did she keep Vivien alive as some kind of weird ghoul? Why didn't she just let her die so she could get what she wanted?"

"Because Vivien wouldn't have died on the full moon. It has to be on the full moon." Tanya scrolled through the newspaper headlines she had photo-graphed. "I looked up the dates of every accident at the Twilight, and every performance has been during a full moon."

Maggie looked over at Kawanna, who had put down her cup of tea, her face ashen. "What's wrong?" Maggie asked her, but Clio's aunt didn't answer.

Rebecca glanced briefly between the two of them, but her attention went back to the papers in front of the girls. "We think the Night Queen has been using Vivien to cause all the accidents at the theater. She's kept her around all this time, stoking her anger, certain that her need for revenge would make her finish the work that Faust started," Rebecca said. "But Vivien never has. She came close, and people got hurt, but she's never brought herself to take a life."

"But that's good, isn't it?" Maggie asked. "It means that Vivien isn't fully under the control of the Night Queen. There's still hope."

"Sure," Clio said. "But things are different this time around."

"Why?" Maggie asked, but before Clio could respond the answer dawned on her. "It's because they're performing *Macbeth*, isn't it? The same play that destroyed Vivien." Maggie imagined what it must feel like for an actress to be forced to watch someone else perform a role that was stolen from her, knowing she would never have a chance at glory. The idea was so painful it almost didn't bear thinking about. "Every time Emily steps on stage, I bet Vivien must see Norma. She sees the person who betrayed her. I know I would."

Clio nodded. "I think you're right."

Maggie took a deep breath. "Okay." Her mind worked, trying to find a solution. "So the Night Queen is banking on Emily being the sacrifice. But maybe if we just stick to Emily and Juniper like glue during rehearsals, they'll stay safe. And as long as we keep everyone out of the theater during the full moon, then we can keep it out of the Night Queen's hands. And after the performance is over we'll just let the city tear down the Twilight like it planned." Maggie turned to Kawanna. "You've been really quiet, Kawanna. What do you think? Could it work?"

Kawanna swallowed thickly. "Maybe," she said. "But there's just one problem."

"What is it?" Maggie asked.

"*Macbeth*'s opening night is Friday." Kawanna pointed weakly to the wall calendar that hung near the register. The square for Friday was circled in bright-red ink, with the words MACBETH OPENING written in all caps. But it was the tiny printing at the bottom of the square that caught the girls' attention.

Friday was also the date of the next full moon.

CHAPTER
18

JUNIPER WAS WITH her father on Monday night, so Maggie didn't have to babysit, but she and her friends went to dress rehearsal just the same. Emily popped by their seats to say hello and deliver a card that Juniper had made. It showed a drawing of Juniper and Maggie holding hands, and inside was scrawled *I miss you! Love, Juni.* "Aww," Maggie said. "Tell that little Junebug that I miss her, too."

"She's already asked if you can come and babysit at our house once the play is finished," Emily said with a smile. "It's not quite as glamorous as the Twilight, but we do have a very good dress-up collection!"

Maggie grinned back at her. "That sounds perfect. I'm in!" Emily slipped away to change into her costume, and Maggie's smile faded. She clutched the little girl's card tightly in her hand, praying she could find a way to keep them all safe.

Nothing unusual had happened during rehearsal, but Maggie sat up in her seat with a gasp every time she thought she caught a flash of red. The constant vigilance had left her exhausted, and her green eyes were tired and strained by the time rehearsal finished and the last few actors gathered their things and headed out. Kawanna waved at the girls, who had moved to a back corner to wait for her.

Kawanna glanced at her watch, which had a beaded rainbow band. "Do y'all mind if I head upstairs to do some quick paperwork before I drop you home? I'll only be about ten minutes." She looked around the theater. "Assuming you feel comfortable being here alone."

Clio looked at the others before answering. "I think we'll be okay. There hasn't been any sign of Vivien."

"See you in a bit." Kawanna disappeared through the double doors to the lobby.

The auditorium was mostly dark, with only the stage lights left on. The big spotlight made a bright circle in the middle of the floor, and the side lights lit the empty set in a cool, blue light.

"That went better than expected," Tanya said softly. "Maybe Vivien realized that she doesn't need to take revenge. Maybe she found a way to move on."

"No way." Maggie thought back to the lonely chamber in the basement, imagining herself trapped inside it for years. It made her chest feel tight, like it was difficult to breathe. "I've seen what she's done. It doesn't seem like she would *ever* get over it." She shook her head. "I used to think I would do anything to be famous. But I can't imagine cheating or hurting another person for it."

No one spoke. Everyone seemed to carry with them the weight of the little stone room and its sad secrets. Suddenly, Clio gripped Maggie's arm. Without speaking she pointed at the stage.

From the darkness of the wings, Vivien Vane crept tentatively onto the stage like a deer into an open meadow. Once the lights reached her skin she lifted her head proudly, and her arms stretched out as if embracing an imaginary crowd. It was Maggie's first clear view of her, and she could see the actress's gown was filthy and tattered by years of wear and grime. Her white gloves had long since turned gray. She carried a bouquet of dead black roses, leaving a trail of dried petals in her wake. She placed the roses gently down at the stage's edge.

Tanya sat up and opened her mouth to speak, but Maggie stopped her. "I don't think she knows we're here," Maggie breathed into her ear. Tanya stayed quiet. Vivien Vane unclipped the veil from her face, and a flurry of moths flew out and up toward the rafter lights. Her stringy hair—or what was left of it—was piled into a colorless rat's nest at the crown of her head. A spider crawled out of her ear and across her face, the dry skin peeled and caked with garish white powder and circles of pasty rouge. Kohl-black makeup rimmed her milky, sunken eyes, and vermilion lipstick was swiped across her bloodless lips in a messy slash.

She gazed upon her imaginary audience, and her mouth stretched open in a smile that cracked the skin of her cheeks and revealed a scattering of tobacco-brown nubs of broken teeth. She looked into the wings as if waiting for her cue, and stepped into the spotlight.

As soon as the light hit her skin, the aged hag melted away, and Maggie was stunned to see a beautiful woman standing in her place: the gown fresh and luxurious, the piled hair now thick and golden blond. Her luminous skin was pale cream, her cheeks flushed with the pink of spring roses. Long, thick lashes ringed her dazzling blue eyes, and her ruby lips opened, revealing perfect white teeth. She took a deep breath and began her monologue.

"*What hath quenched them hath given me fire . . .*" As Vivien spoke the lines of the mad queen, she paced the stage, moving in and out of the spotlight, her face and body transforming with every shift between light and shadow.

Maggie looked over at Tanya, who was frantically writing in her notebook, her eyebrows so high on her forehead they almost disappeared. She couldn't see the others, but she imagined they were just as stunned as she was.

Vivien finished her monologue and stepped forward, bowing deeply to her imaginary crowd of admirers. She reached down and picked up the discarded bouquet as though it had just been thrown to her by an adoring fan. She held it to her face and buried her nose in the blooms. She took another deep bow and blew a kiss to the audience before she swept into the wings and disappeared.

Maggie held her breath, waiting to see if Vivien would come back. When the stage remained silent and still a few moments later, Maggie turned to her friends. "Guys, I think Vivien is getting ready for something. She's rehearsing."

"Yeah, but for what?" Tanya asked.

"Emily's part." And Maggie knew there was only one reason the ghoul would still be rehearsing the part of Lady Macbeth. It was because Vivien didn't plan for Emily to be around to perform it.

CHAPTER 19

THE NEXT MORNING during break, Maggie and her friends stood shivering in the covered courtyard, talking about the events of the previous night. Maggie felt a tap on her shoulder and turned around. Val and Nobi stood behind her, Val dressed all in black with a pair of heavy engineer boots and a battered men's overcoat, its lapels encrusted with buttons and pins. Nobi slouched next to her, wearing red skinny jeans and a frayed *Dear Evan Hansen* T-shirt under a pinstripe blazer. His spiky hair stood at attention, each individual lock molded to a perfect point. Maggie's face broke into a surprised grin. "Oh, hey!"

"Hey," Val said with a shy smile. "We haven't seen you at the library lately."

"Yeah, sorry," Maggie said. "I thought you guys might not be so psyched to see me after I got your hopes up with the whole petition thing. Sorry I wasted your time and everything."

"It's not your fault. Since when has this school ever listened to the students?" Nobi shrugged. "It was worth a try anyway."

"Thanks," Maggie said. She introduced Nobi and Val to her friends.

"Are you guys going to see *Macbeth* at the Twilight this weekend?" Val asked. "Nobi and I got tickets for opening night this Friday. I hear it's going to be amazing!"

Maggie and her friends looked at one another uneasily. "Yeah, we'll be there," Maggie said.

"Cool! See you later." Nobi and Val headed off with a wave.

"Oh, great," Maggie said. "Now we can add my new drama friends to the list of people to worry about on Friday night. Sounds perfect!"

"At least Juniper won't be there," Tanya said.

"Yeah, it'll be way past her bedtime," Maggie answered.

"It's really cool that Emily found a sitter to stay with her at home so you could still come to the show," Rebecca said.

"For sure," Maggie said.

"I wish my aunt would just cancel the *Macbeth* performance," Clio said. "But she won't. She says that no one is going to listen to her if she tells them she has to cancel a play because of a curse. The actors have put in too much hard work. What are we going to do?"

Maggie pulled the zipper of her fuzzy pink coat all the way up to her chin and yanked her faux-fur hat down over her ears. "The Night Queen is using Vivien's anger to bait her into doing something to Emily." Maggie couldn't bring herself to say out loud that Emily might die. It was too frightening to think about. "So, basically, Vivien *is* the Twilight's curse. She's been the cause of all the tragedies at the theater. If we find a way to stop Vivien, then we find a way to stop the curse, right?"

There was a long silence, and Tanya shoved her hands deeper into her coat pockets. "Let's hope so."

·····

Dark clouds obscured the full moon as Maggie and Clio stood outside the theater on Friday night taking tickets and watching all the guests walk in. Maggie was worried about Vivien's curse, but she couldn't help but be drawn in by the glamor of the theater's grand reopening. Kawanna had brought her sense of flair to the evening. A red carpet led from the sidewalk to the front doors, and she had set up a decorative backdrop on one side, where a photographer from the *Piper Register* was taking pictures of posing guests.

"Wow," Maggie said. "It's just like a real premiere." She pointed to the backdrop. "That's called a Step and Repeat, because at big movie premieres and stuff, there are so many paparazzi that celebrities have to take a step, pose, and then keep repeating it all along the red carpet." Maggie put her hands on her hips and angled her body slightly to one side, showing off her leopard-print flats and marabou-trimmed emerald trapeze dress. "What do you think?"

"Obviously you're a natural. That dress is super cute," Clio said. "The green really sets off your red hair." Clio was also dressed up for the occasion in a bright-yellow dress with a turquoise statement necklace and matching flats. Her hair was pulled up in a bun that sat on her head like a crown.

"I'm feeling really nervous," Maggie admitted. "I mean, our only plan to protect Emily is to find Vivien and capture her before she can hurt anyone. What if we can't find her? And what about the Night Queen? This plan has more holes in it than swiss cheese! What if it doesn't work and something happens to Emily? It'll be our fault."

"Nothing's going to happen to Emily," a voice said behind her. Maggie turned to find Rebecca dressed in a short black dress with a white collar and cuffs. She had on black suede high-tops, and her hair was in two braids. "Sorry I'm late. My brother had a meltdown just as we were leaving, so my parents decided to stay home. My mom just dropped me off." She lowered her voice. "Have you guys been inside yet? Anything strange going on in there?"

Maggie shook her head. "I got here early and helped Emily get into her costume, and things have been quiet so far. I left her in the greenroom running lines with some of the other actors."

"What's a greenroom?" Rebecca asked.

"It's like a little backstage lounge where the actors relax and hang out when they don't have to be onstage for a while." Maggie glanced at her watch and eyed the crowd of people still waiting to get into the theater. "We should get back inside and check on things."

"You and Clio go ahead," Tanya said. "Rebecca and I will take over here and meet up with you in a few."

"Thanks," Maggie said. She and Clio hurried

into the crowded lobby. A throng of people stood in line at the old glass concession stand, manned by volunteers from the Piper Preservation Society. A sign on the counter said ALL PROCEEDS GO TO RENO- VATING THE THEATER. Maggie bit her lip, and her eyes wandered to the ram's horns in the balcony's grill- work. A few weeks ago she would have done anything to see the theater returned to its former glory, but now she hoped the city would tear it down. She hated imagining the Night Queen hovering just out of sight, watching and waiting for the chance to open up a permanent portal from the Nightmare Realm, so she and her *lusus naturae* minions could come pouring through.

"Let's check backstage first," Maggie said. "That seems like the most likely place for Vivien to strike." As she walked through the doors to the auditorium, Maggie caught a glimpse of red in one of the balcony boxes and let out an involuntary cry. A closer look revealed a young woman in a red jumpsuit squeez- ing against her boyfriend for a selfie. "Sorry," Maggie said. "False alarm."

They picked their way down the aisle, stepping carefully around the dazzled theatergoers who were oohing and aahing at every stunning detail. "I can't believe I've walked by this place every day for years and never had any idea what was inside," Maggie overheard someone say. *If only you knew*, Maggie thought to herself. She glanced at her watch again. "This is taking too long."

"Side door," Clio answered. She grabbed Maggie's wrist and ducked through a doorway that led to a wide carpeted hallway. Most of the guests had elected to come through the main doors, so the corridor was empty.

Clio and Maggie pulled open a door that said BACKSTAGE ENTRY. AUTHORIZED PERSONNEL ONLY. A burly crew member in a black T-shirt went to stop them, but he recognized Maggie and let them through. "Have you seen Emily?" Maggie asked.

"She's standing in the wings." He pointed to the figure in a long red gown and matching veil over her face, standing in the half shadow of the curtain. Maggie caught her breath for a moment. *Relax*, she told herself. *That's Emily's costume. You helped her get dressed yourself.*

Maggie started toward the wings. "Emily! We came to tell you to break a leg!" Instead of waving back, the figure shrank into the shadows. Emily and Clio looked at each other and hastened their steps. By the time they reached the curtain, the figure was gone.

Clio's voice was low. "Not Emily."

"I need to go make sure the real Emily's okay," Maggie said.

Clio's phone buzzed and she pulled it out. "Rebecca and Tanya are coming in. I'll go ask my auntie to get them backstage. I'll meet you outside the dressing rooms."

Maggie raced toward the dressing rooms, peering up to check the empty rafters as she passed behind the closed curtains. Would she be able to stop Vivien before she could strike? How could she keep Emily safe without telling her about the curse?

Maggie passed Alan, who was checking himself in a backstage mirror, dabbing extra spirit gum on his fake gray beard and bushy eyebrows before sticking them on. "Hey, Alan. Have you seen Emily?"

Alan pointed back toward the dressing rooms. The door to the women's dressing room was closed. There were almost no other women in the play, and she prayed that Emily hadn't been left alone. There was no answer when Maggie knocked, so she burst open the door.

A red figure stood in the center of the dressing room, her long, white gloves dripping with blood.

CHAPTER 20

"MAGGIE! THANK GOODNESS you're here," the figure said. "I was checking to make sure I had enough fake blood, and I spilled it all over my gloves."

Maggie breathed a sigh of relief. It was Emily. "I'll see if we can find a fresh pair," she said, carefully taking the gloves off one at a time. She sent a quick text to Clio, asking her to get a spare set from her aunt. She looked around the empty room. "Where are the other actresses?"

"Kawanna had a few pizzas delivered to the greenroom, so they went to grab a bite." Emily flipped her veil up over her head, revealing deep-red lips, dark-rimmed eyes, and shadows dusted under her cheekbones. She looked eerie and not at all like the fresh-faced young mother Maggie had come to know. "I always get too nervous to eat before a show, and I was happy for a few minutes alone, anyway. It's good to have some time to concentrate and get myself in character."

"Cool." Maggie knew she should give Emily her space, but she didn't want to leave her alone. Not until she was sure Emily was safe for now. She scanned the room, looking for signs that Vivien had been there. At first glance, everything seemed ordinary. A long, black-tiled vanity ran along a mirrored wall, with simple folding chairs lined up along it. Gym bags and totes stuffed with the actors' street clothes were shoved underneath. A rolling steel rack holding costumes for quick backstage changes was pushed near the door, and Maggie shuddered inwardly, remembering Vivien's dressing room prison. She thought of the Night Queen's secret nook in the basement and peeped behind the rack. No hidden shrine. Good.

There was a knock at the door, and Maggie jumped. She opened it to find Clio holding out a pair of long, white gloves. Rebecca and Tanya stood behind her. They shot her a questioning look, and Maggie gave them a quick nod to show that everything was all right. "Aunt Kawanna asked me to tell Emily that the curtain opens in ten minutes," Clio said quietly.

"Okay, I'll let her know," Maggie said.

Clio's voice dropped even lower. "We'll be out here. Tanya's going to check out the catwalk, and Rebecca and I will chill in the wings."

Maggie shut the door and handed Emily the gloves. "Ten minutes," she said.

Emily looked at the clock on the wall and took a deep breath. "Oh, wow. The time sure went fast." She rubbed her hands together nervously. "This is my first play since Juniper was born. I hope I still know what I'm doing."

"Are you kidding?" Maggie asked. "I saw you in rehearsals and you were amazing. I've learned so much just by watching you."

Emily smiled gratefully and pulled on the gloves. "I just want everything to go smoothly, you know?"

"I'm sure it will," Maggie said, hoping she spoke the truth. She wished she could warn Emily somehow, but the actress was already anxious enough. And what would Maggie say, anyway? *Oh, by the way, break a leg, and try not to get killed by any angry ghoul women tonight!* That wouldn't exactly go over well ten minutes to curtain.

Emily checked her face in the mirror and applied a fresh coat of lipstick before reapplying her veil. That's when Maggie noticed the bouquet. Red roses in a tall, jet-black vase. Maggie knew exactly where she had seen that vase before. "Who sent you these?" she asked.

Emily glanced over. "I don't know, actually. I've been so busy I haven't had a chance to read the card."

Just then, the dressing room door opened and an actress wearing a ragged dress and wild, black wig swept in. Maggie recognized her as Helen, the retired zookeeper, who was playing one of the witches. "It's time, Emily. All actors need to be in the wings." She turned around and swept out again, practicing her witchy cackle.

Emily stood up. "Well, I'm off." She smiled at Maggie. "Whatever you do, don't wish me luck!"

Maggie laughed. "I promise I won't." She knew that theater superstition considered *Good luck* to be one of the unluckiest phrases an actor could ever hear. "Break a leg." Emily blew her a kiss and left in a swirl of nervous energy.

Maggie turned back to the bouquet and picked up the card with a sense of trepidation. She slipped it out of the envelope, already recognizing the red edging along the heavy, cream card. There was no signature, but the words were written in the familiar elegant scrawl: *Good luck tonight. Always treat each performance as if it were your last.*

· · · · ·

The curtain had just opened by the time Maggie had met up with her friends and showed them the card. She knew they needed to find Vivien, and fast. The other girls had checked backstage and all the balconies, so that left the theater's lower levels.

Walking downstairs from the hustle and bustle of the main floor felt like walking into a ghost town. Although the restrooms were open to the public for the performance, the other rooms weren't in use for the evening. The play had already started, so they didn't see another soul as they crept quietly through the unused spaces. The old restaurant and ballroom doors were chained shut and secured with heavy padlocks, so they passed both rooms by and continued their search.

"I still can't believe you and Juniper *played* down here," Rebecca whispered. "Even without Vivien lurking around, it's just so creepy!"

"Maybe," Maggie answered. "But it probably wouldn't feel that way if it were full of people."

"Yeah," Rebecca said, "but it *isn't*. You were

always down here alone, with all this spooky old stuff where anything could be hiding." She shuddered. "I think I prefer my buildings shiny and new, thank you very much."

The girls came upon an oak door with a brass inlay of an owl on it. The sign above read OWL BAR. "The theater was built during the Prohibition era, but they still had a bar?" Clio asked. She pushed open the door to the empty Owl Bar and flipped on the lights. The oak-paneled room was tiny, with just a few small cocktail tables and a marble-topped bar.

"They claimed it was just for smoking cigars and drinking sarsaparilla," Maggie said, "but Kawanna says the room is full of hidden panels and drawers where customers could hide their hooch in case of a raid."

"See, normally I would think that hidden panels and stuff were cool," Clio said, "but tonight, not so much."

Maggie peeked behind the bar and caught a whiff of ancient cigar smoke, but no perfume.

"Not much room to hide," Rebecca said. "At least, not that we can see." She turned to Tanya. "Should we get out the net and stuff? We need to be organized and ready when we find Vivien."

"No way." Maggie tapped the walls, searching for hidden panels. "If she sees us carrying a net, we won't get within fifty feet of her. We have to keep it hidden until the last possible second." One of the panels felt loose when she tapped it. She pushed it harder, and it sprang open, revealing a dusty old wine bottle and a few cloudy glasses. "I just hope we get to her before the Night Queen pushes her over the edge."

"How does the Night Queen even talk to Vivien anyway? The portal to the Nightmare Realm has never been open here, right?" Tanya looked under one of the tables. No one there. She pressed a button and a drawer popped open. It was empty.

"Good question," Clio answered. "But that awful clock at the Lees' wasn't a portal, either, and we still don't know what that thing was for. Maybe she used something like that."

"There's nothing here," Maggie said. "Let's keep moving."

They checked the empty ladies' lounge next. There was a loudspeaker in the vanity area so showgoers didn't have to miss any of the performance. Maggie listened. "*But screw your courage to the sticking place and we'll not fail . . .*"

"That's Emily's voice," Maggie said. "So far so

good, but the first act is almost over. We're running out of time." She led them out of the lounge and over to the last empty room on the floor: the nursery. She pulled open the door and clicked on the light.

It was every bit as grim as she remembered, with its dark olive carpet and depressing circus mural, but Maggie felt an additional uneasiness as her eyes searched the room. Something was different. She walked over to the dollhouse. All the dolls had been returned, and someone had set it up to look like the evening's performance, with several dolls in the audience seats and a few more onstage. Maggie looked for the blond doll, the one that Juniper had pretended was Emily. It was missing.

Across the room near the puppet theater, Rebecca stood near a tiny, child-sized door that Maggie hadn't noticed on her earlier visits. The door had a shiny new padlock on it. "What's in here?" Rebecca asked.

"I don't know," Maggie said. "I don't remember seeing it before." She walked over to take a closer look. There was a fresh smudge of mossy green on the rusty hasp. Maggie locked eyes with Rebecca.

"Are you thinking what I'm thinking?" Rebecca asked.

Maggie nodded. "We need to find out what's behind that door."

"Tanya, we have to get this open. Do you have your crowbar?" Rebecca called.

"Not tonight. I just brought stuff for capturing, not exploring." Tanya rummaged through the toy boxes for something she could use as a tool. Maggie grabbed at the lock and tugged, twisting it in the hopes that the old wood would give behind the hasp. A hairline crack formed in the wood, and Maggie gave a grunt of satisfaction.

Just then, there was an unearthly screech from the puppet booth, and puppets exploded into the air. Something flew at Maggie, knocking her to the ground, and she screamed. Maggie could hear the other girls rushing to her aid as she struggled against the sinewy arms that grabbed at her. "Help!" Maggie shrieked. "What's happening?!"

Rebecca's firm, authoritative voice cut sharply through the melee. "Horrible! What are you doing?! Stop it!" Her attacker's grip slackened, and Maggie's eyes finally focused on the hideous creature in front of her. The size and general shape of a spider monkey, Horrible was far less cute, with his ropy arms, mushroom-tipped fingers, and the black taloned feet that sprouted from his stumpy legs. The torn onesie on the changeling's rotten-log body was filthier than ever, and his caved-apple face held an expression of anxious resentment.

Maggie looked at him with disgust. "What's he doing here?! I thought we were rid of that thing forever!" Horrible snapped at Maggie and climbed into Rebecca's arms. "Oh, come on, Rebecca, don't tell me you're going to *hold* him now! Gross! I hope you're planning to burn that outfit when you get home tonight."

"Oh, he's not so bad," Rebecca said, looking down at him. Horrible and Rebecca held a special bond ever since she had accidentally become his unwitting babysitter a few months back. Discovering that Horrible was a changeling is what led them to their first encounter with the Night Queen, and Rebecca had ended up saving his life. "But what *are* you doing here, Horrible? Is it something to do with this?" She reached for the lock again, and Horrible smacked her hand away. She looked more closely at the streak of green moss, the moss that matched the streaks on Horrible's body. "Wait a minute, did *you* put the padlock on here?" Horrible nodded and tugged on her hand, pulling her away.

Clio slowly backed up toward the exit. "You guys, Horrible only seems to show up when the

Night Queen's nearby, so maybe we really *don't* want to find out what's behind that door."

Maggie looked at her watch and stood up. "Act Two is already halfway over; we'd better get back upstairs and check on—" As she turned to leave, the rest of the sentence died in her throat.

A figure loomed in the doorway, blocking their exit. Her tattered gown hung on her bony frame like a scarlet burial shroud.

They had found Vivien Vane at last.

CHAPTER
21

MAGGIE WAS SO frightened she couldn't make a sound. Her insides were gripped with fear, but also a strange kind of relief. As long as Vivien was down here with them, then Emily was safe. And as long as Emily was safe, then the Night Queen couldn't open the theater's portal. *Unless . . .* Maggie thought. *Unless the Night Queen convinced Vivien to go after us instead of Emily.*

Vivien's face was obscured by her veil, but Maggie could see the two dark circles of her sunken eyes, their gaze seeming to burn Maggie's skin with long-held fury. Her gloved hands were curled like claws in front of her.

The other girls gathered around Maggie, and

Horrible cowered in Rebecca's arms. "Well, we've been looking for her all night, and we found her." Tanya slowly put her backpack on the floor. "Now how do we . . . you know, *apture-cay er-hay?*" she asked, slipping into Pig Latin in the hopes that Vivien wouldn't catch on.

"Follow my lead," Maggie whispered. She took a step forward and cleared her throat, trying to will her hands to stop trembling. "Vivien Vane, it's an honor to meet you. We've been reading all about you, and you're a legend."

The face behind the veil shifted, and Vivien's posture changed. Her hands softened. Maggie heard Tanya quietly unclipping her backpack, but Maggie was careful not to look at her. She made sure Vivien's eyes stayed locked on her own.

Maggie went on. "It takes a lot of talent to go from chorus girl to featured performer, and you were awesome in that film footage we saw." The actress stood up straight and put one hand against her heart. From the corner of her eye, Maggie saw Tanya and Clio take a few steps to one side, carrying something between them. It was working! The girls took another cautious step forward.

Suddenly there was a hiss from across the room, and a peal of laughter that sounded like ice-cold bells. Terror shot through Maggie's heart. That laugh still wove through her nightmares.

The Night Queen was here.

Maggie's panic turned her plan to dust. She tore her gaze from Vivien and wheeled around, expecting to see the blue woman towering behind her, but there was no one there. Then Maggie saw it: the mirror in the corner. There was something moving behind the glass. Maggie caught a glimpse of golden falcon eyes, the silver curl of a ram's horn, and the restless movement of arachnid legs.

Horrible hopped out of Rebecca's arms and cowered on the floor, shaking uncontrollably. He crept toward the mirror as if dragged by a chain. Rebecca pulled at him. "Horrible? What are you doing?" He looked back at her with a pleading look and pressed his face into the floor, still inching closer to the Night Queen's reflection.

Maggie turned back to Vivien, hoping to regain her attention, but the dark pits of her eyes watched only the mirror now. Maggie willed Clio and Tanya to make their move, but the girls were just as frozen as she was, standing like statues with the net stretched limply between them. The queen's voice rang through the room, and Horrible curled up like a ball, covering his head at the sound of it. "Don't let this false flattery try to take from you what's yours. They care nothing for you! Destroy them and find the revenge you seek."

Her words seemed to shock Maggie back to herself. "Vivien!" Maggie cried. "Don't listen to her. I've seen your work, and you're an incredible performer. I hope someday I can grow up and be as talented as you!" Maggie was surprised to find that the words were true. Whatever ghoulish thing Vivien was now, she would have been a true star if things had turned out differently.

Vivien looked back at her with questioning eyes. Almost hopeful. She wanted to believe Maggie. She wanted to listen. "Please, Vivien. Talent is your legacy, not revenge."

Maybe they wouldn't need the net after all. Maybe she could get Vivien to trust her. Maggie kept her gaze on Vivien's face, hoping the other girls would understand and back off. In her peripheral vision, she saw Tanya and Clio look at each other and bring their arms down. The net sagged. They had understood! "Trust me," Maggie said.

The queen's icy voice cut in, dripping with scorn. "Trust them?" Her eyes blazed in the mirror. "They seek to stop you, to imprison you." Her voice lowered, sounding almost hypnotic. "They would trap you in obscurity forever . . . just as Norma did." Vivien's body went rigid, and she shook her head in confusion. "Behold," the queen commanded. "See for yourself what they would do."

"No!" Maggie said. "That's not true!" She cast a frantic eye at Clio and Tanya, praying they had put away the net, but the two girls still stood there like two deer caught in headlights, the drooping net held loosely in their hands. Vivien followed Maggie's gaze and turned on the two girls, letting out a shriek of rage. She tore the net from their hands. "Wait, no!" Maggie cried. "Please! It's not what you think!" But Vivien was blind to Maggie's pleas now.

The queen pushed her advantage. "No one cares for you the way I do, Vivien," she purred. "While others would see you suffer and vanish from the earth, it is I who will give you what you want." Her voice grew louder. "At last you will have the revenge and the fame you were denied all these years!" The frigid voice sliced through the nursery like a scythe. "Now, awake, sleeping ones! Arise and crush them all!" Horrible writhed in agony on the floor, shrieking and clawing at his ears.

The little door in the wall began to rattle, the handle turning violently. The padlock rattled. The door shook harder, the wood beginning to crack.

Rebecca threw herself against the door, trying to keep it shut. "Help me!" she cried. Clio ran to her, but Vivien grabbed Tanya by the arm, lifting her until her toes barely touched the ground. Tanya screamed.

"No! She's a liar!" Maggie shouted. Tears streamed down Tanya's face as Vivien raised her free hand to strike. "Stop! The queen is the reason you suffered! She kept you alive so she could use you! She could have saved you but she didn't!" Maggie's words seemed to reach her, and Vivien loosened her grip. Tanya broke free and fell to the ground. She scurried backward, and Maggie stepped protectively in front of her.

"Please don't do this," Maggie said. "This is not who you really are."

Vivien dropped her hands to her sides, clenching and unclenching her fists. Then she turned on her heels and fled the nursery, locking the door behind her.

CHAPTER
22

THE QUEEN'S TRIUMPHANT laughter curdled the room. "Did you worthless mortals really believe she would listen to you? No twisted monster I bring to life can ever defy me; I am their creator!" Her golden eyes glittered, and her voice dropped to a vicious hiss that could barely be heard over the rattling of the door. "Isn't that right . . . changeling?"

Horrible had been creeping across the carpet, searching for a hiding place, but at the sound of his name, he froze. "Come to me, changeling. Come to your maker." Horrible crawled to the mirror.

"No!" Rebecca cried. "Don't go to her!" She pulled at him, but he shook her off. He hunched before the mirror, trembling violently.

"Now, show them what you are, changeling.

Remove the lock. Let in those I have freshly awakened. Let them take what is theirs." Whimpering and dragging his taloned feet, Horrible went to the little door. He reached into his mouth and pulled out a silver key. The rattling stopped.

"Horrible, stop! What are you doing?" Rebecca grabbed at him, but he slithered out of her grasp. Maggie heard the key click in the padlock, and it fell to the floor with a thud.

The door opened, and Maggie stood in horror as one after another, three skeletons poured into the room. "*Lusus naturae!*" Rebecca cried. "They're from the Nightmare Realm! She must have opened the portal!"

"You weak fools! To think I am only served by creatures from the Nightmare Realm? I have the power to awaken all that rest uneasy in the earth and bend them to my will forever. There is no escape!" The skeletons carried hammers and crowbars in their bony hands. It was the builders—the ones who had disappeared during the theater's construction. They advanced on the girls, brandishing their weapons. Horrible scuttled to the far corner of the room, cowering by the dollhouse.

"We can't fight them!" Tanya cried. "We have to get out of here!" The girls ran to the exit, pushing

in vain at the door, but it was no use. They were trapped.

"Now, awakened ones. Finish them!" the Night Queen cried. A skeleton raised its hammer above Rebecca's head.

Horrible let out a shriek. He picked up the dollhouse and hurled it at the mirror, shattering it. Shards of silvery glass spilled out, littering the floor like fallen stars. The whole building shook on its foundations, and the skeletons fell to the floor, the bones scattering across the carpet and turning to dust.

"What just happened?" Clio cried.

"No time to find out!" Maggie shouted. "We have to save Emily!" She grabbed a crowbar from the floor and banged it against the doorknob. Nothing happened. She let out a scream of frustration.

Tanya ran over and took the crowbar out of her hands. "Not like that. Like this." She wedged the end between the handle and the jamb and rocked it back and forth until the door snapped open. She grinned. "It's amazing what you can do with the right tool!"

"I love you, T, but stop talking," Maggie said. "Let's go!" The girls followed Maggie upstairs and through the backstage door. A figure in red stood in the wings, watching.

"Tackle her!" Clio whispered.

Maggie pulled her back "No!" She held up one hand. "Wait." She walked slowly over to the woman in red.

"Maggie," the woman said. It was Emily. "How's the play going so far? Are you having fun?" She took one look at Maggie's pale, tearstained face and stopped. She lifted her veil and bent down, putting her hand on Maggie's shoulder. "What happened? Are you all right?"

Maggie looked across the stage, past where Malcolm, the dead king's son, rallied his troops to overthrow the wicked Macbeth. "*Our power is ready; our lack is nothing but our leave. Macbeth is ripe for shaking, and the powers above put on their instruments. Receive what cheer you may. The night is long that never finds the day.*" On the catwalk above she saw another woman in red staring intently at the action below.

"I need to talk to you," Maggie whispered. She saw Vivien's head turn, and she felt the ghoul's eyes on her as she took hold of Emily's hand.

"Is there any way it can wait? I'm about to do my final scene, and then I can give you all the time you need."

Maggie shook her head, and tears spilled down her cheeks. "It can't wait." She took Emily's hand

and looked pleadingly up at her. "Please don't do your final scene."

Emily's eyes followed the actors playing the other parts on stage, and turned back to Maggie. "Can you at least tell me why not?"

Maggie bit her lip. "I can't explain. Just please don't do it. Please." Her friends gathered around them, forming a protective circle.

"Maggie, I have to go on. I don't have an understudy, and this is one of the most important scenes in the play."

Maggie took a deep breath. "Emily, I'm asking you to trust me, just like I'm trusting you. Just stay here with me, please. It's for your own safety. I promise you it will be all right."

Emily's eyes were clear as she looked down at Maggie. "Okay. I trust you." She let Clio and Maggie lead her to a folding chair near the rear curtain. Maggie looked up at the catwalk. It was empty. Had Vivien understood?

Emily's cue came and went, and no one appeared on stage. Maggie's stomach twisted. The actress playing the maid spoke again, her voice louder. "*Lo you, here she comes. This is her very guise . . .*" Vivien entered the scene from the other side of the stage carrying a lit candle. Maggie tensed. What if the other adults weren't able to see her? Vivien crossed the stage in silence. The other actors shifted their positions, adjusting to the last-minute blocking change, but they continued in stride. Maggie breathed a sigh of relief. It had worked.

Vivien paced the stage, every inch the mad queen. She stood in the spotlight and looked down in horror at her bare hands, the skin young and fresh again in the light's glow. *"Here's the smell of the blood still. All the perfumes of Arabia will not sweeten this little hand."* Maggie held her breath, gripped by the performance. Vivien truly was a star. Maggie felt a pull in her heart when she thought about all that could have been.

The play continued, and Maggie went back to Emily. Emily squeezed Maggie's shoulder. "What a talent! Where did she come from?" Maggie didn't answer.

They watched the rest of the play from the wings, and when it came time for the curtain call, Emily went to stand, but Maggie grabbed her hand and pulled her back to her seat. "Not yet," she said.

When Lady Macbeth took her bow, it was Vivien, not Emily, who swept forward to receive the crowd's adulation. The crowd roared as the spotlight shone down upon her, and roses—fresh, red roses—landed

at her feet. Vivien took a final, sweeping bow, and her red gown and veil collapsed like a paper lantern, hollow and empty. A scattering of dust and dried rose petals sifted across the stage, and even from the wings Maggie could smell a whiff of perfume. The startled cast jumped backward, but the audience roared even louder, thinking the actress's disappearance was part of the show.

But Maggie knew better.

Vivien had become a star at last.

CHAPTER 23

AS THE CURTAIN began to close, Emily gripped Maggie's shoulder tightly, her face pale. "What just happened? Who was she?"

Maggie took both of Emily's hands in her own and looked intently in her eyes. "She was you, okay? That was *you* on stage. You did the whole show, and you and Kawanna planned a magic trick at curtain call to give the show a little more buzz. Do you understand? You have to say that it was you."

"And if I don't?" Emily asked, eyes wide.

Maggie shrugged. "No one will believe you."

Emily looked at the four girls. "I don't know what just happened, but I have a feeling I should thank you." She touched Maggie's cheek and hurried off to greet the cast as they walked off stage. "What did you think of our little magic trick?" Maggie heard her ask, as the rest of the cast buzzed excitedly around her. Emily really was a terrific actress.

"Should we make sure my auntie knows the little cover story you just concocted?" Clio asked. "And tell her how the nursery got trashed?"

Maggie grimaced. "Oh, yeah. We should probably go talk to her."

It wasn't hard to find Kawanna. She and Irene, the director, were surrounded by a crowd of admirers. Kawanna had changed out of the simple black clothes she wore backstage and into a vintage 1920s gold-beaded gown with a matching silk head scarf. Sparkling gems dangled from her ears and at her throat, and she looked like she had walked straight out of an old Hollywood movie. Gone were the anxious lines around her face. Her coppery cheeks were glowing with happiness. When she saw Clio and the others coming, she waved to the crowd, saying, "Now, you know a good magician never reveals her secrets!" and ducked away to join the girls.

Kawanna led them downstairs into a quiet corner where they wouldn't be overheard. "That was some curtain call," she said. "I guess that means you were successful?"

"Yeah," Maggie said. "But things got a little . . . complicated." She and the other girls filled Kawanna in on what had happened as they walked her to the nursery. The dollhouse sat in a broken heap in the corner, and shattered mirror glass lay scattered across the floor. Horrible was nowhere to be seen. The little door in the wall hung open on its hinges, a crumbled hole behind it. "What do we do about all of this?"

Kawanna nodded slowly as she looked around the room, thinking. "I'll figure something out." Her face curled with distaste as she eyed the hideous murals and sad, claustrophobic ceiling. "I tell you, this has got to be the worst nursery design in history." The girls all laughed. "For now, let's collect this broken glass, and we'll figure out the rest at the shop tomorrow."

The girls carefully swept up the mirror shards and collected them in a cardboard box. "Where do we keep them?" Maggie asked. "I don't think we should leave them here."

"Well, I don't want them in my house," Rebecca said.

"Me neither," Clio added.

Tanya picked up the box. "I'll take them; I don't mind. I'd like to study them." She carried the box out, and the other girls followed. The crowds were starting to thin out, but Maggie could hear people lingering upstairs in the lobby, still raving about the opening night success.

Maggie took one last look at the dark nursery. It had been a close call, but they had done it. They had broken the Night Queen's power over the Twilight. The curse had been broken. She turned away and into the golden light where her friends were waiting.

· · · · ·

The next afternoon, Maggie stood eagerly behind the Creature Features counter. For once in her life she was the first to arrive, and she wasn't about to waste the opportunity. Maggie hovered next to a white cardboard box that she had placed next to the empty silver platter that was usually loaded with doughnuts. The CLOSED sign was on the door, but a moment later the front bell chimed as Clio, Tanya, and Rebecca piled into the store.

"Where's my auntie?" Clio asked, sliding her backpack off and folding her wool peacoat on top of it.

"She went to get the tea," Maggie said. "She'll be back in a sec."

Rebecca pulled off her puffy down jacket and

hung it carefully on the coat rack near the door. "What's that?" she asked, eyeing the box.

"It's a surprise," Maggie said, trying to hide her smile.

Tanya tugged off her fingerless gloves and unwrapped the multicolored striped scarf from her neck before tossing both on the floor. "I love you, Mags, but I don't know if I can handle any more surprises."

The girls heard footsteps coming down the hallway from Kawanna's little apartment at the back of the shop, but something sounded wrong. They could hear a low wail that grew louder, and Kawanna burst through the doorway, her hand wrapped in a bloody dishrag.

"What happened!?" Clio cried.

"I was cooking, and the knife slipped," Kawanna moaned. "I think I need to go to the emergency room!" She unwrapped the bloody dish towel, displaying a single brown finger, cleanly cut at the base.

Rebecca screamed. "Quick! Apply pressure!" She grabbed a handful of napkins from the countertop.

"We need ice!" Tanya yelled. She ran toward the doorway to Kawanna's apartment and bumped into the wall.

Maggie turned green. "I think I'm going to pass out," she wailed.

"Hold up." Kawanna closed the towel again. "I think I'm feeling better. Let me check again." She put the bloody dishrag on the counter and opened her hand. It was completely unharmed. A familiar twinkle appeared in her eye, and a grin stretched across her face.

"Are you kidding, Auntie? You were *pranking* us?!" Clio swatted her aunt's shoulder. "Not. Funny."

Rebecca shook her head and clucked her tongue disapprovingly. "That has got to be your worst prank yet."

Maggie collapsed against the counter. "I know, right? I seriously almost barfed!"

Kawanna unfolded the dishrag and held up the rubber finger. "New inventory. Just came in this morning! Pretty cool, huh?"

"No," Tanya said flatly, and everyone laughed. It was good to see Kawanna back to her old self again.

Kawanna wiped her hands on a spare napkin. "The fund-raiser was a huge success. I feel like a giant weight's been lifted off my shoulders. The mayor found me last night, and he said the council decided that the theater is worth keeping. They aren't going to tear it down, so it looks like the Twilight is finally safe."

"That's awesome!" Maggie said. She shifted uncomfortably. "But is the theater, you know, *safe* safe? Like safe from the Night Queen?"

Clio smiled and pulled a small red book out of her backpack: *Tales of the Night Queen*. "I think so. Listen to this:

> *In Queene's fair fist her servant held*
> *To her dark will is he compelled*
> *If servant can the Queene defy*
> *Then foul will fall and hope is high*
> *Her power fades like morning dew*
> *And joyful life begins anew."*

The others' faces broke out in huge grins, but Maggie was still in the dark. "Um, in English, please?"

"The poem says that whatever the Night Queen creates must obey her, but if any of her minions can break free of her will, then it strikes a crucial blow to her power, bringing hope and new life back to the places she once held," Kawanna explained.

Maggie blinked. "Oh. Wow. So Vivien and Horrible *both* helped save the day? I never thought that little stinker was anything but trouble." She took a deep breath. "I know I'm going to regret saying this, but it looks like you were right about him, Becks."

Rebecca tossed her braid behind her shoulder. "You should know by now, Mags, I'm pretty much right about everything." Maggie laughed and rested her head against her friend.

"Rebecca wasn't the only one who got it right," Clio said. "Maggie, how did you know that letting Vivien perform would break the curse?"

Maggie thought for a moment. "I know it sounds funny, but that night when we caught Vivien rehearsing, I saw something in her face. Her expression was—I'm not sure how to explain it—but it looked . . . like there was a piece missing from her, and then she found it again. I just knew she needed that missing piece. She deserved a chance to get it back."

Kawanna's warm brown eyes looked at Maggie with deep affection and pride. "I knew you were just the right person for the job, Maggie. I'm so, so proud of you."

Maggie beamed. She reached for the white box and carefully opened up the lid. "That reminds me, I ordered a little something special today." The girls gathered round as Maggie unboxed a beautiful cake decorated to look like the Twilight's facade.

CONGRATULATIONS, KAWANNA! was written across the marquee. She looked at Rebecca. "I hope you're not mad that I didn't ask you to do it, Becks, but I wanted to surprise everybody."

"Are you kidding?" Rebecca asked. "There's no way I could make something this good!" She grinned. "Not yet, at least." She leaned closer to examine the detail on the icing. "Where did it come from?"

Maggie smiled shyly. "I bought it with my baby-sitting money."

Kawanna's eyes were damp. She put a hand on Maggie's shoulder. "Thank you, honey. That means a lot." She looked up as the bell at the front door jangled. "And I sure am glad you brought this cake, because I invited a few extra guests today!" Ethan waved as he walked into the shop, followed by Emily and Juniper, and finally Nobi and Val.

Maggie's face lit up, and she ran over to give them all hugs. Juniper gave her an extra squeeze. "I missed you, Juni B!" Maggie said. She ushered everyone in, and Rebecca started slicing and serving up cake as Emily and Kawanna disappeared to the back to bring out the rest of the food.

Maggie was pleased to see Nobi and Val were already chatting with Ethan and Clio, while Tanya crouched down next to Juniper, nodding at something the little girl was saying. Maggie looked at her expanding circle of friends and felt a burst of pride. She may not be as brainy or organized as they were, and her drama club project had been a hopeless flop, but she knew how to help people, and she knew how to be a good friend. Juniper ran over and hugged her legs. *And I'm a pretty good babysitter, too*, Maggie thought.

Emily laid platters of crackers, cheese, and cut-up veggies on the counter, and Kawanna poured juice into snakeskin-patterned paper cups. After a few moments she clapped her hands, and the room grew quiet.

"Maggie's not the only one with a surprise today," Kawanna said. She and Emily exchanged a secret smile. "Dr. Gujadhur came up to Emily and me after the show last night, and mentioned that a certain *persistent* young lady and her friends had petitioned him to start a drama club." Maggie felt her cheeks grow hot, remembering the stack of signatures sitting uselessly on his desk. "In fact, he said it was a shame that Sanger Middle School can't host the club, so he asked if Emily might be willing to start a youth drama program at the Twilight."

Maggie's eyes widened. "Really?! No way!"

Kawanna's eyes sparkled. "Yes way! And that's

not all. Your principal was so impressed with your efforts that he even offered to speak to the town council about using some of their arts funding budget to pay for it!" Maggie, Nobi, and Val screamed and hugged one another. Then they ran over and hugged Emily and Kawanna.

Kawanna gave Maggie a high five. "You must have made *quite* the impression on him!"

Maggie laughed and struck a pose. "Well, if there's one thing I know, it's how to make an impression!"

. . . . .

A few months later Maggie and her friends wandered the Twilight's fully restored lobby. The nursery was still under construction, but the rest of the theater's renovations were nearly complete. Maggie had been visiting the Twilight a lot in the past few weeks, and it no longer felt like a terrifying place that filled her with dread. In fact, it was starting to feel a little bit like home.

She led her friends across the lobby to where a large sign said CELEBRATING A FORGOTTEN LEGEND. Beside it were a few glass display cases and some framed pictures on the wall. "Kawanna and I have been working on this," she said. "What do you think?" The exhibit held costumes, keepsakes, clippings, and photos, all in celebration of the lost work of Vivien Vane. Maggie pointed to a gold compact and matching lipstick tube. "This was her signature lipstick color, Phantom Red. The color was created just for her, you know."

"This is incredible," Val said, admiring the exhibit. "It's almost like you really knew her."

Maggie and her friends shared a secret smile. "Yeah, it kind of feels like I did."

Before they walked downstairs to check out the new restaurant, Maggie peeped her head into the dark auditorium.

There, in the middle of the stage, stood the ghost light, shining once more. The lamp glowed in the darkness, guiding all lost spirits safely home again.

EPILOGUE

THE BELL JANGLED on the door of the old junk and salvage warehouse just outside of Piper. The proprietor looked up from his fishing magazine and wiped a hand across his bushy white mustache. "Can I help you?"

The couple looked around. "Maybe," the woman said. Bakelite bangles clattered down her wrists as she pushed her gray-streaked dark curls out of her face. "We're both artists, and we make sculptures out of repurposed materials. We're just looking around, hoping to get some inspiration."

"Hmm," the old man said. "Can't say I know much about that, but I will tell you we just got a shipment of new stuff from Piper. They're renovating that old movie palace out there. Could be a few things from that haul might interest you." He led them over to the back of the warehouse near the cargo door. "Haven't had much chance to go through it, yet, so feel free to poke around." He stood nearby as the couple picked through the broken velvet seats, the old film projector and canisters, and a few other odds and ends.

Suddenly, the woman let out a cry of delight. "Oh, Eli, come see!" She was bent over a wooden crate of broken mosaic tiles in shades of silver, white, and midnight blue. She held up a piece. "Look at the detail on this! Is that a woman's face?"

The man came over for a closer look. "Extraordinary!" He reached into the crate and rummaged around, hissing as he cut his finger on a single shard of mirror that was mixed in with the tiles. He picked it up. "This looks like part of an old diamond dust mirror." He held it to the light, and something flashed in it, golden like a falcon's eye. "It's awfully cloudy. It must be really old."

"This is perfect," the woman said. She looked up at the proprietor. "How much for the whole crate?" He named a price, and she pulled out her wallet. "We'll take it."

The woman picked up the crate. "I think this will be our most memorable creation yet."

Acknowledgments

The Los Angeles Theatre was the crown jewel of the movie palaces that lined Broadway in downtown LA. Completed in 1931, this architectural masterpiece was open for only a few months before its owner filed for bankruptcy, and the theater closed later that same year. This was the inspiration for the fictional Twilight Theater of this story. You can read more about its fascinating history at http://www.losangelestheatre.com/history. I first explored the theater in much the same way Maggie discovered the Twilight: wandering the floors and exploring its near-empty rooms, none of which had yet been renovated. My imagination went absolutely wild, and I fell in love with every inch of that magical place. I am forever grateful for the Broadway Theater Group and City Councilmember José Huizar's Bringing Back Broadway initiative for working so hard to restore, protect, and preserve buildings like the Los Angeles Theatre.

My love for both drama and abandoned buildings started young. My mother worked as an actress, and her theater troupe was one of the first to rent out practice space in an abandoned high school that was being converted to an arts center. I owe her, as well as the Maryland Hall Story Theater, a debt of gratitude for letting me tag along to rehearsals, where I learned so much about acting and directing and urban exploring.

Life as a working writer continues to challenge and excite, and I am ever appreciative of all of you who tenderly cheer us on. Brava to my peerless agent, Erin Murphy, who sets a standard of integrity and kindness that regularly leaves me in awe. She also does a masterful job of attracting an exceptional gaggle of writers that it is a blessing to know. I adore each and every one of you in my EMLA family, but I especially want to thank Elly Swartz, Jason Gallaher, Jennifer Ziegler and Chris Barton, Debbie Michiko Florence, Lori Snyder, Christina Uss, Anna Redding, Ann Braden, Hayley Barrett, and Maria Gianferrari for your incredible warmth and generosity as I muddled my way through my debut. And the longer I work with Imprint, the more I delight that this series has found a home here. A standing ovation for Erin Stein and Nicole Otto; it is a dream to collaborate with you, and I thank you from the bottom of my heart for your thoughtful shepherding of this series, and of me. Much applause also for Rayanne Vieira, Natalie C. Sousa, Kelsey Marrujo, and the whole Imprint and MacKids team.

Heartfelt thanks to Monstrously Good Middle Grade and all my fellow spooky authors for making horror so much fun. My continued gratitude to Jarrett Lerner, Corrina Allen, and all the folks at MG Book Village for continuing to champion the books our middle graders need. So many roses flung onstage to #bookexpedition, #bookvoyage, #collabookation, and all the other ARC-sharing groups for sharing, loving, and promoting books and literacy. Educators like Erin Varley, Susan Sullivan, Rosy Burke, Jason Lewis, Michele Knott, Kristen Picone, Andrea Childes, Rebecca Reynolds, Patrick Andrus, Miss Nikki, and all the folks at nErDCamp keep authors inspired and remind us why we write. Footstomping hoots and hollers for independent bookstores like Red Balloon and Tattered Cover, who make every author feel welcome and loved. I am also grateful to Barnes & Noble for all the support it has given to me and this series.

And finally, I'd like to thank my treasured friends and family for keeping the ghost light burning for me near and far, with cameo appearances by Jane Leo, Rebecca Anderson, Mary Jo Scott, the HYDIAS crew, Julie Maigret, Kathi Chandler-Payatt, Brenda Winter Hansen, Sarah Azibo, and Kevin Maher. And to my forever costar, Eddie Gamarra, and our ensemble cast of dogs, the spotlight of my heart shines always on your cherished faces. Beloved, beloved, beloved ones, I thank you.

About the Author

KAT SHEPHERD loves to create fast-paced adventure stories that are likely to engage reluctant readers because she wholeheartedly believes that reading should be a joyful experience for every child.

A former classroom teacher, Kat has also spent various points in her life working as a deli waitress, a Hollywood script reader, and a dog trainer for film and TV. She lives in Minneapolis with her husband, two dogs, and a rotating series of foster dogs. Babysitting Nightmares is her first middle grade series.

katshepherd.com
babysittingnightmares.com